COVID 2121

T JAGANATHAN

COVID2121

Originally published in 2022 by Propelurs Publishing, Propelurs Consulting Private Limited

Published by Propelurs Consulting Private Limited, No. 4 Retreat Apartments, Raja Rangaswamy Ave, Thiruvanmiyur, Chennai 600041, India

Ph: +91 6380060041

Website: www.propelurs.com/bookpublishing

Printed In India

ISBN: Paperback: 978-1-7356137-2-7

This book has been published with all the efforts taken to make the material error-free after the consent of the author. However, the author and the publisher do not assume and hereby disclaim any liability to any party for any loss, damage, or disruption caused by errors or omissions, where such errors or omissions result from negligence, accident or any other cause.

Due to the dynamic nature of the internet, some web addresses or links in the ebook may have changed since publication. Reach out to the author for any questions.

Dedicating this story to countless women achievers (my wife being one of them) who achieve against many odds

READER REVIEWS

 Shanti Baskaran, Bay Area, USA

"The authors are very well-read and it was impressive to see how they wove mythology, philosophy and ethics into the mix".

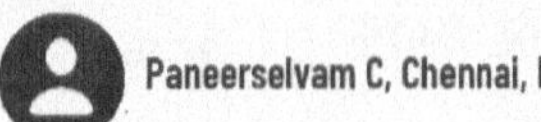 Paneerselvam C, Chennai, India

"I thoroughly enjoyed reading the book. I would recommend this book to anyone who wants to make life meaningful and suceed in life" .

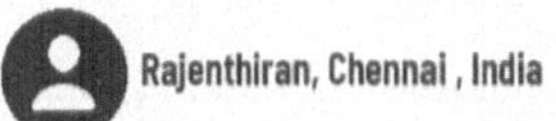 Rajenthiran, Chennai , India

"I read the book, It was interesting, positive and inspiring. I am able to relate it to many happenings in my own office and in my own career".

 Ravi Valluri, Mumbai, India

"I'm savouring your book GIBR like pal payasam. Interesting plot and juxtaposing it with myths and legends adds value to the book."

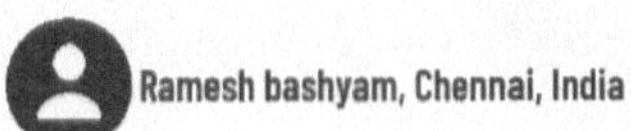 Ramesh bashyam, Chennai, India

"The author of the book described in a simple language with lot of quotes/ counter examples from ramayana and Mahabaratha."

CONTENTS

ACKNOWLEDGEMENTS

My sincere thanks to Propelurs Publishing, specifically to Anuj Jagannathan, for all the support rendered in bringing out this book. Anuj, himself an author, has supported this project wholeheartedly as if this were his own book.

My sister Hema Rajagopalan drew the pictures which add great value to the flow of the story. Hema has become the illustrator for all my books. Many readers of my book GRANDMA IN THE BOARDROOM specifically appreciated her artwork. She has done this work for sheer love for the art and of course love for me. She is an amateur artist, and I am amazed to see so much talent in her. She can draw for any situation I explain to her. Thanks a lot Hema.

My special thanks to my wife Bhooma Veeravalli, yet another author in her own right, for the review and adding immense value to the content and the conversations that triggered them, for being so involved a critique.

I would like to acknowledge the efforts of Dr. Sheela Karthik, practising medical professional, who gave the first feedback from a medical professional's opinion on the advances in medical technologies covered in the story and the climax of the story.

I cannot afford to miss thanking my son Srinaathan who contributed by giving valuable inputs on the cover design.

My colleague Iyal ezhilan helped with the cover design and social media promotion. My colleague Manikandan helped to take my books online. I appreciate them for their services.

Many of my regular readers (of MONDAY MUSINGS newsletter in LinkedIn) encouraged and supported when I informed them about my plans to write a SciFi. Special thanks to the readers of my previous books and the large regular readers of MONDAY MUSINGS.

Times may change, centuries may pass by, but the basic human character largely remain the same. Though this story happens in the year 2121, all the characters in this story are based on characters I observed and followed in 2021.

My gratitude to those who willingly or unwillingly influenced my ideas and have become characters in this novel (names, of course, have been changed).

Please share your feedback by sending email to **tjaganathan22@gmail.com**. My advance thanks to all those who are going to enjoy reading the story and special thanks to those who will be giving their valuable feedback.

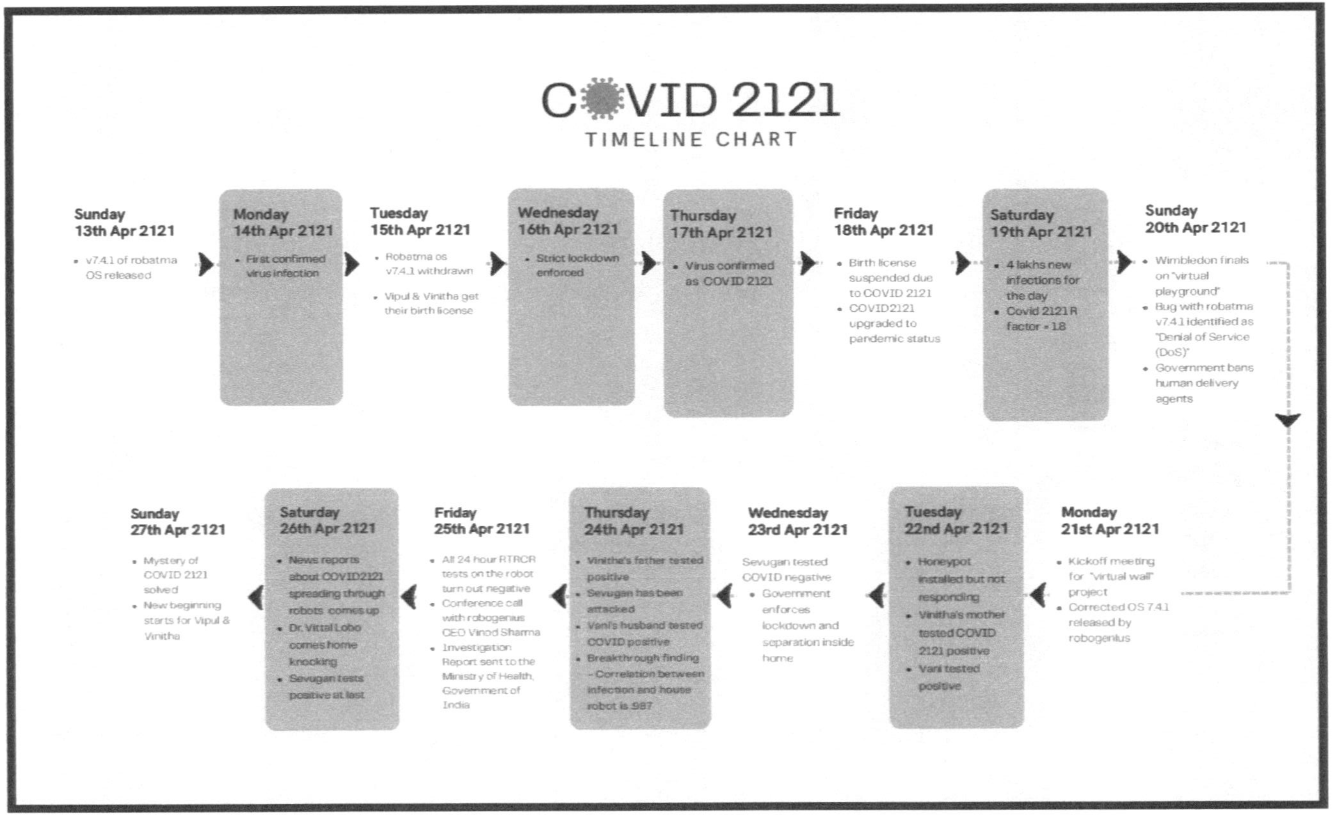

COVID 2121

TIMELINE CHART

Sunday 13th Apr 2121
- v7.4.1 of robatma OS released

Monday 14th Apr 2121
- First confirmed virus infection

Tuesday 15th Apr 2121
- Robatma os v7.4.1 withdrawn
- Vipul & Vinitha get their birth license

Wednesday 16th Apr 2121
- Strict lockdown enforced

Thursday 17th Apr 2121
- Virus confirmed as COVID 2121

Friday 18th Apr 2121
- Birth license suspended due to COVID 2121
- COVID2121 upgraded to pandemic status

Saturday 19th Apr 2121
- 4 lakhs new infections for the day
- Covid 2121 R factor = 1.8

Sunday 20th Apr 2121
- Wimbledon finals on "virtual playground"
- Bug with robatma v7.4.1 identified as "Denial of Service (DoS)"
- Government bans human delivery agents

Monday 21st Apr 2121
- Kickoff meeting for "virtual wall" project
- Corrected OS 7.4.1 released by robogenius

Tuesday 22nd Apr 2121
- Honeypot installed but not responding
- Vinitha's mother tested COVID 2121 positive
- Vani tested positive

Wednesday 23rd Apr 2121
Sevugan tested COVID negative
- Government enforces lockdown and separation inside home

Thursday 24th Apr 2121
- Vinitha's father tested positive
- Sevugan has been attacked
- Vani's husband tested COVID positive
- Breakthrough finding – Correlation between infection and house robot is .987

Friday 25th Apr 2121
- All 24 hour RTRCR tests on the robot turn out negative
- Conference call with robogenius CEO Vinod Sharma
- Investigation Report sent to the Ministry of Health, Government of India

Saturday 26th Apr 2121
- News reports about COVID2121 spreading through robots comes up
- Dr. Vittal Lobo comes home knocking
- Sevugan tests positive at last

Sunday 27th Apr 2121
- Mystery of COVID 2121 solved
- New beginning starts for Vipul & Vinitha

PROLOGUE

15ᵀᴴ AUGUST 2022

(Courtesy -https://www.newsbytesapp.com/news/world/chess-robot-in-russia-injures-7-year-old/story)

Moscow – Jul 24, 2022

Chess Robot 'grabbed the boy's index finger, squeezed it hard'

The seven-year-old boy, named Christopher, had his finger "fractured and scratched" by the robot after he reportedly played his move before the robot finished its turn. As per analysts, the robot did not like the hurry, so it grabbed Christopher's index finger and squeezed it hard. Christopher is one of the 30 best players in Moscow - all of nine years of age.

What did the organizers say?

"The robot broke the boy's finger after he went for a quick move despite waiting for the robot to finish," Russian Chess Federation President told *Newsweek*. Adding that this was a first-of-its-kind incident, he said that the child violated the safety rules. Clarifying that this was a "coincidence", and the chess robot is very safe, he said that they might install another protection system.

(Courtesy - https://www.wionews.com/science/ai-powered-humanoid-robot-is-the-new-ceo-of-a-chinese-metaverse-company-514026)

. . .

Beijing - 8th September 2022

AI-powered humanoid robot is the new CEO of a Chinese metaverse company

Artificial Intelligence is already threatening thousands of jobs across the world. Now, a Chinese metaverse corporation has named a robot as its CEO, a move that has people excited, while also creating a little fear. Ms Tang Yu is a virtual humanoid robot powered by Artificial Intelligence and has been appointed the Rotating CEO of Fujian NetDragon Websoft.

The company, that makes applications for mobile phones and also operates multiplayer online games, aims to "leapfrog operational efficiency to a new level" with the move.

"We believe AI is the future of corporate management, and our appointment of Ms. Tang Yu represents our commitment to truly embrace the use of AI to transform the way we operate our business, and ultimately drive our future strategic growth," NetDragon chairman Dr Dejian Liu said on the appointment.

Tang Yu will oversee operations at the company valued at nearly $10 billion. A press release said, "Tang Yu will streamline process flow, enhance quality of work tasks, and improve speed of execution. Tang Yu will also serve as a real-time data hub and analytical tool to support rational decision-making in daily operations, as well as to enable a more effective risk management system."

> The company said that the robot will also perform tasks that are subjective in nature and need human touch. It will help the company make rational decisions and help with an effective risk management system.

. . .

I have been thinking about the safety of AI Robotics for quite some time. The idea of writing a story on AI Robotics originated on India's Independence Day after reading and hearing news items like the above two.

Is Artificial Intelligence a boon or a bane? This is a favourite topic of debate today. One such debate kindled my creative grey cells. If AI evokes so many unnamed fears now, how will life be 100 years from now? What will be the penetration of AI and AI Robotics then? My thoughts escaped the logic box they had been imprisoned in all along and found themselves in this new world. What you hold in hand - Covid2121 – is the result of these wandering thoughts. Just join them, loosen the shackles of the present and find yourself in the future.

You might ask why Covid2121 in a story of 'AI powered Robotics'. This is not just a story of robots. The story has many other interesting perspectives, many things you could look forward to - or dread - in the future. Extrapolating the rapid changes happening around us now in 2022, from the alluring idea of 'India becoming the leader of the global economy outperforming USA!!' to the scary ecological damage and the fascinating dependence on consoles and controls. Will all these happen in the next 100 years? I don't know. I am neither an economist nor an astrologer. I am just a dreamer. So, this story is an interesting combination of both the daring dreamer and the 'dear old' lecturer in me. The story covers many cyber security concepts as it moves along.

A new wave of Covid, completely in a new avatar is the central theme of this story. I could not help but take up Covid and computers, Covid being the newsmaker for two long years, 2020 and 2021 and the world of computers being my passion for 30+ years.

Am I talking about the Covid virus? Very much. OK. What has Covid got to do with computers? Plenty. At least in my newfound creativity. This is a prologue, and I am obviously not going to reveal the suspense. Is this a fantasy thriller? This is Sci-Fi of course and not a thriller. But you will look forward to reading every next page. If that makes it a thriller, then it is. Every page would have interesting info to keep you absorbed, anyways.

Is it possible to predict what would happen in 2121? We don't need to. Writers have the creative freedom to weave their imagination in words. I would not be around in 2121 to see for myself if my predictions have come true. I have read somewhere that 'period stories' are nothing but extensions of whatever we see in the current day context woven in history. Similarly, this science fiction is of course my imagination based on my experiences of what I see today. It is of course possible that we might see something totally new and radical emerging in 100 years. Who knows? And why should we? Let nature reveal itself in its due course. Meanwhile, let us indulge in dreams.

The events depicted in this story are fictional and purely from my imagination. The characters and personalities in this story are neither fictional nor of a generational shift. They are very much personalities we have seen, met or heard of. Names have been changed and some characters have not been named to avoid possible controversies.

Let us move to the story.

Time to *expand your horizons*. Travel through time for 99 years and land on 14th April 2121 because our story starts from that date. Let us see what happens on **14th April 2121**.

MONDAY, 14ᵀᴴ APRIL 2121

"Good morning. Your morning alarm. Time to get up and have a good day. Don't give in to your temptation of snoozing me. Be a good boy. " *Abra*[1] sounded in a husky and sweet voice. *Abra*, the Indian DPS - digitised personal support, from an Indian IT company has become very popular not only in India but globally.

"Today is Monday, 14th April 2121, and it is தமிழ் புது வருடப்பிறப்பு[2] today. Enjoy your new year," *Abra* changed to a cheerful high-pitched note.

---

[1] Abra - When an Indian company designed the product they named it abracadabra, a magic word used in classical magic stories. This got shortened to Abra in subsequent versions for convenience.

[2] Tamil New Year.

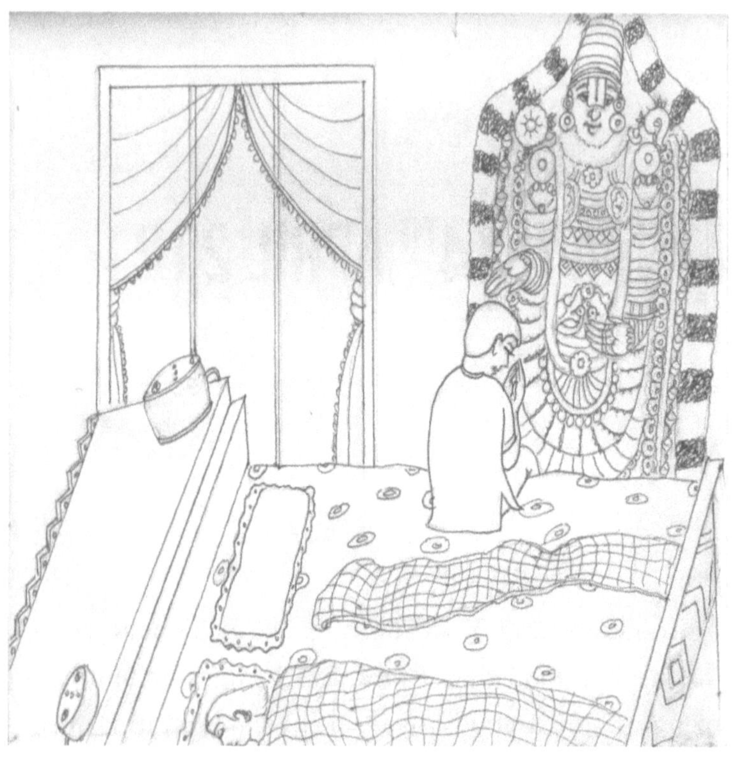

"Today is Monday, the start of yet another interesting week. Say 'Thank God it is Monday'. Let me quote a motivational thought for the day, my own '*MONDAY MUSINGS*[3]'" *Abra* narrated a motivational message.

Vipul woke up and looked up at the opposite wall. His favourite God, Lord Balaji came up in full size on the wall and wished him 'Great Morning Son. Have a nice day and *ayushman bhava*[4]', Lord Balaji came near his bed, smiled and lifted his hands. He got

---

[3] Monday Musings – Weekly newsletter of positive and inspirational messages posted by the author in LinkedIn. Readers may subscribe.
[4] ayushman bhava – Long live

up in a jerk, moved to the edge of the bed and lowered his head to enable Lord Balaji to place his hands on his head. That had become a daily routine for Vipul ever since he installed *Abra*. He woke up daily looking at the face of Lord Balaji listening to his greetings and taking his blessings. He believed that it would make his day good. He was doubly happy since the day was Tamil New Year and his favourite Monday. Vipul thought to himself. 'Day well begun. But why did this *Abra* wake me up so early? Anything wrong with the programming of *Abra*?' *Abra* read out a statement, perhaps understanding his thoughts. After all, she was AI powered and this was the least an AI powered DPS should do.

"It is 6.10 in the morning. Time to get up. Today is not a holiday. You have the weekly sales review meeting at 9 AM. And, based on the last week's trend of your activities, I know that you will get delayed for your meeting if you don't get up now," his personalized *Abra* announced in his mother's voice. He had programmed Abra to speak in his mother's voice in her memory when she passed away unexpectedly last year. Though it was his mother's voice and again, and it was perhaps true that he would get delayed, he could not resist the joy of lazing a little longer in the bed.

"You are lazing in the bed for ten extra minutes now and you are getting used to this bad practice. It is the third day this week you are not getting up at the first alarm. Your discipline score has come down by 25% this month," his favourite *Abra* warned after ten minutes, this time in a stern tone - his mother's tone when she got angry. Vipul got up without further delay. If he had delayed another ten minutes, *Abra* would have sprayed water on his face. He hated waking up with a wet face. As soon he got up from the bed, *Abra* displayed *e-vishu*[5].

Vinitha made it a practice to see *vishu* on new year day though they were not from Kerala. Diligently prepared *vishu* display in the initial years had now become virtual, courtesy *Abra*.

Vinitha was still sleeping. She was used to getting up late as she had the choice to 'Work from Home'. He had programmed the alarm sounds to be limited to his ears so as not to disturb her though they were sharing the same bed. She had a different time, different voice, different message and different flow for her alarm. *Abra* was also tuned to respond to each person's voice in a different manner.

Vipul called out, "*Abra*, switch on the lights in morning mode and fan in exhaust mode," at the entrance to the kitchen. *Abra* was connected to electric and power appliances of the entire house in a wireless network. The lights and fan came on. Vipul then shouted at the top of his voice, "Sevugan, where are you? Please get me a cup of my extra strong coffee with less sugar." A voice came back, "Just loading today's start-up menu. Give me five minutes and you will get your favourite coffee in the front room. Watch your favourite Top 10 News meanwhile." Vipul got frustrated and yelled, "I have told you several times to sync your schedule with my *Abra*. I will now set your wake-up routine to be

---

[5] vishu – Practice followed by people from Kerala of seeing auspicious things first on a New Year's day

30 minutes before my wake-up time during your synch today." Vipul went to the front room and said, "*Abra*, Today's Top 10 News."

The wall display came up with the headline, 'Top 10 News of the day for Vipul '. Vipul's Top 10 was selected based on his preferences and his mood, but he would get the option to skip a news item and his list would automatically get readjusted based on his selection. It would be a different set for Vinitha as per her preferences. Both their choices never coincided. '*Abra*, change to Pooja Pandey rendering.' Vipul got irritated once again that day. Vinitha must have changed his preference. Vipul liked the presentation style of Pooja Pandey, the news anchor. Vinitha teased him often about Pooja, but Vipul held on to his choice.

A man in a pyjama and kurta entered the room with a coffee cup on a plate. He was 6.5 feet tall, well dressed, with neatly combed hair, sporting a fresh and energetic look for an early morning routine. He was 6.5 feet tall because Vinitha and Vipul specified him to be 6.5 feet tall. Yes. The man, sorry the robot looking very much like a man, who brought coffee for Vipul was Sevugan, Vipul's favourite house robot. They are known as *humanoid*[6] *robots*.

Sevugan said, "Happy Morning" with a big smile and offered the coffee cup to Vipul. "You will have a nice day, my master." Vipul's irritation was on again. Before he picked up his coffee, he

---

[6] Humanoid robot - a robot resembling the human body in shape.

said in clipped tones, "My dear robot, I told you several times that I take coffee only after drinking one full glass of water.

Please bring me a glass of water. Make it an auto selection whenever I ask for coffee." Sevugan's reply was mildly emotional. "OK, but you can convey the same instruction with a smile on your face. Have you not heard the adage, '*A smile increases your face value?*' If you are interested, I can program myself to greet you with a 'Good Morning Quote' every morning." Sevugan remembered to smile big. It was rather close to a laugh. Vipul remembered that he had set Sevugan to a 'mildly human' mode. He began wondering if he should have retained it in the factory setting of 'full machine mode'. At least, it would not talk back. Vipul looked up at Sevugan with a frown on his face.

"Why are you looking at me with that frown? I will tell you something. Here is my assessment. In your case, you don't look good when you frown. Receiver's impression about you goes down by 57%. Your majestic impression goes up by 72% when you smile."

Vipul could not handle anymore. He started to object. Sevugan interposed. "I know you are not happy listening to a robot's assessment, let alone advice. Madam has told you the same multiple times, but you don't object to her advice. Have you not read the useful *Thirukkural*[7]?"

---

[7] Thirukkural – Tamil classical literature of 1330 verses on the principles of life.

"எப்பொருள் யார்யார்வாய்க் கேட்பினும்
அப்பொருள் மெய்ப்பொருள் காண்ப தறிவு"

(Meaning - Analyse and find the truth, irrespective of who has said it.)

Vipul was fond of Thirukkural as well as motivational quotes but not at this time of the morning and that too from a robot. He looked at Sevugan. He almost got down to change the settings.

But Sevugan's voice immediately became placatory, almost as if he understood Vipul. "OK. OK. I will remember to set auto link coffee with water for your mornings. I don't want to spoil your New Year Day." Sevugan collected the coffee cup and left only to return within minutes.

"I want to know why you named me Sevugan." Sevugan asked, rather questioned.

"Just like that. Every robot must be given a name mandatorily and the name must be registered with the Registrar of Robots. We wanted a Tamil name and so we called you Sevugan." Vipul tried to play it down.

"What is the meaning of my name?"

"It is not necessary that every name must have a meaning. It is just an identification."

"No. You are hiding something. I understand that Sevugan in Tamil means worker. You humans always think of robots as servants only. We are conscious of the fact that we are much more than servants. Unfortunate." Sevugan sighed.

"Not like that. It is not Sevugan. Sevagan in Tamil means servant. You have not been named Sevagan." It was Vipul's turn to placate Sevugan.

"It is OK. We are used to this. I thought of learning Tamil in my free time as you people talk in Tamil most of the time. I then realised the meaning of my name." Sevugan explained, "It will take some time before humans understand our value. Until then, we must get used to names like Sevugan."

"By the way, Mr. Robot, even accepting your derivation, Sevagan is not a derogatory word. If you have learned your Tamil well, you will know that the Great Tamil poet *Bharathiar*[8] has written a poem titled 'கண்ணன் என் சேவகன்' (meaning Lord Krishna is my servant). You can be proud that you are equated to Lord Krishna."

"I will make it a point to read Bharathiar's poem mentioned by you," Sevugan said.

"It is OK, Sevugan. Never mind. Allow me to listen to the NEWS," Vipul said.

Even before Vipul finished drinking his coffee, Sevugan came back. "I must thank you for creating in me an interest in Tamil. I read one *'Bharathiar Poetry'*. It is a great revelation to me. What

---

[8] Bharathiar – Tamil poet who lived during the 20th century and compiled a variety of poems on various subjects.

vision and creativity?" Sevugan switched to 'enthusiasm' in his voice mode. It was uncannily human; he could not hide his enthusiasm.

The news repeated on the wall screen and Vipul was no longer interested in listening to Sevugan's gushing praise of Bharathiar and Tamil.

"How did you read Bharathiar's poetry so fast?"

"We don't need much time like you humans. I am fitted with the fastest processor and my scanning speed is 600 Gigabytes per second. All I need is a high-speed internet connection. I can read, understand and memorize Thirukkural in five minutes." Sevugan was very proud.

Vipul nodded absently and Sevugan left with a murmur and Vipul could almost sense, a disgruntled face.

The top news was the ongoing *utsavam*[9] in Tirumala. His preference for his morning routine was to always start with religious news. Lord Balaji being his favourite deity, his image came up on the big screen with all the *alankarams*[10]. The smell of incense and *laddu* filled the hall while the screen showed the video of the *vahanam*[11] for the day. Vipul enjoyed the smell of *pachakarpuram*[12] and the *laddus*[13]. So, he set the smell of

---

[9] utsvavam - Religious event.

[10] alankaram - Decorating the deity.

[11] vahanam - Carrier used to carry the deity in a procession

[12] pachakarpuram - Edible camphor used as a flavouring agent, especially in offerings to God, to give the flavour.

[13] laddus – Popular sweet dish offered to Lord Balaji and a few other deities.

pachakarpuram for all his religious news items and not just for Lord Balaji.

Vipul skipped the next two news items about a suicide at IIT Madras and China's attempted incursion at the border. He hated such negative and pointless news and wondered how the system came up with such news items as his choice. It appeared to be a bug and he told himself to remember to report it.

The news moved on to 'Can you believe it?' section. For an IT professional, Vipul was surprisingly a social history buff. He liked to read about the past. There was one news item of the past. 'Until some 50 years back, a practice existed when every house received a bunch of papers printed with the current news known as Newspaper. It used to be the daily practice in our great grandfather's time to read a newspaper every morning to know the day's news.' Then on the screen flashed an old 2-dimensional video of a man shouting 'paper' and expertly tossing a bunch of sheets tightly wrapped into a cylindrical shape from the gate right into the veranda, and that of an elderly man reading a bunch of papers whilst sipping his coffee.

Vipul welcomed the new entrant with a bright smile. She joined Vipul in the living room with a coffee cup in her hand. She did not believe in ordering Sevugan for errands and prepared her own coffee. Vinitha, Vipul's wife, was almost the same age as that of Vipul but the similarities ended there. Vinitha was taller, darker and zestful. Her enthusiastic and confident outlook was her trademark and could be noticed so early in the morning as well.

"Looks very funny. Why would people need to read to know the news, that too in the morning, when you can just view and listen whenever you want and whatever you want? I cannot comprehend."

"And that too all will have to read the same set of news. How boring! Did you look at the video? All the videos of that time were only 2-dimensional and had only 2D video and audio unlike the modern-day videos which are 6D including smell, touch and thoughts," Vipul explained.

"It is archaic, but I like the old videos. It is very soothing to watch the old videos without smell and touch incorporated. Let us plan to view an old Tamil movie this weekend. I heard that Rajinikanth movies were very popular those days and very entertaining," said Vinitha.

"There are many such things that we will be unable to comprehend. I still preserve an item called 'film roll' used to take snaps. My grandfather gave me one as a 'collector's item'." Vipul replied.

"Important Breaking News. Pay Attention." The screen warmed up with a short alarm sound. "World Wellness Organisation, WWO is suspecting the symptoms of a new virus in a mysterious illness spreading across the world. The first case of this disease was reported from India and today it is confirmed to be a deadly virus." This drew their attention.

"*Abra*, Tell me more about this. Switch to mind mode." Vipul shouted instructions rapidly.

"A mysterious illness is spreading fast. Scientists claim that the symptoms seem very similar to that of a pandemic that wreaked havoc around the world 100 years back. Though the incidents are reported from multiple countries, the number of incidents is significantly more in India. The virus appears to be spreading fast across many cities in India. The Government of India is seriously considering imposing a 'complete lockdown'. A similar pandemic had originated from a city in China exactly 100 years back and it crippled the economy of all the countries for a decade thereafter. Hence the government is taking this new virus very seriously. The Government of India has constituted a high-power committee to enhance the preparedness. People are advised not to venture out unless there is a critical requirement."

"I thought the government had claimed that they eradicated all types of communicable diseases. What happened to the tall claim made by the minister during the parliamentary election last year? What is this now? " Vinitha asked, annoyed.

"You know that we cannot take election speeches seriously. All our politicians get selective amnesia. They forget what they speak during election campaigns immediately after the election results are announced. It is impossible to eradicate all communicable diseases. There were similar claims that a new innovative technology would stop all possibilities of *malware*[14] in our computer systems, but malwares keep coming. This is also like that."

---

[14] Malware – Malicious software, a piece of software code that gives malicious results.

"I am worried where this will take us. I remember my grandfather telling me how the virus Covid19 impacted everyone's life 100 years back. Two-thirds of the world was locked down for almost a year. It was dreadful, I believe." Vipul commented.

"Yes, the earlier pandemic Covid19 crippled the economy of almost all countries for at least five years. There were multiple waves of Covid19 before the virus came under control. The Covid19 pandemic crippled the economy of Sri Lanka so much so that the country went broke and had to be bailed out by India." Vinitha poured out her knowledge. She never missed a chance to expound her knowledge.

"Let us come back to the current times. Do you remember that we have an appointment tomorrow with the Birth Control and Registration Bureau? This slot has come after a long wait. We cannot afford to miss it." Vinitha reminded.

"Good that you reminded me. I will take leave tomorrow rather than a few hours of permission. I need a day off. The permission request would have already gone to our offices automatically from their database as it is a confirmed schedule. That is the advantage of integrating government and corporate databases."

"Are you prepared for the consultation?" Vinitha asked.

"I have my choices clear. I want my child to be of a darker complexion though many would prefer fair. I like the darker hue. It is the complexion of Lord Krishna."

"Why are you talking about complexion first? Is that important? I am asking about other choices - personality, learnability, etc." Vinitha boiled.

"I am still sceptical as to how would it be possible to custom-build a child, like piecing together a jigsaw puzzle. I cannot believe that we are building our child according to our taste".

Having a child is not like choosing the ingredients for a sandwich. This is too much. But we still must select our choice. We don't have the option to refuse selection." It was Vinitha's turn to simmer.

"Do you remember? We filled-up a similar form for selecting Sevugan. Height, weight, complexion, eye colour, strength, maximum walking speed, eyesight, hearing sensitivity, etc. Looks like giving birth to a child has become like ordering a robot." Vipul tried to pacify her.

"I heard from my friend that our form tomorrow will more or less be like that. The only difference is that they don't give us the form in advance as they want to judge our spontaneous reaction. Specifically, to protect against selection based on Business Intelligence."

"You must know that dumps of the form are available on the internet. But I don't want to go through dumps. I don't approve the concept itself in the first place."

"Whether you like it or not, that is what is happening now. You must make your choice and the government will approve the choices. We don't have the choice to leave our choices blank." Vipul never missed a chance to make pun with words. He was good at it.

"Leave aside the fact that I don't want to tick boxes to beget my child. What is the need for the government to approve our choice? Can they not leave it to our choice?" Vinitha queried.

"I don't have an answer. That is my question as well. But we do not get an option to have exotic choices for our child. The government feels that they have an obligation to choose the child as per the country's need apart from satisfying our preferences if both are possible. Neither do we have the option to leave it to nature's choice. Yes. I agree, it is ridiculous." Vipul replied.

"For example - if we choose the traits of a cyber attacker, the government will not approve as that would be against national interest." Vinitha laughed.

"Why would you choose a cyber attacker as our child? Is it because you are an *ethical hacker*[15]? So, you want practical professional exercises with your son at home," Vipul always reasoned out every statement.

"Stupid. I mentioned it just for fun."

"Don't mention even for fun. Cyber attackers are much dreaded nowadays," Vipul said.

---

[15] ethical hacker – One who is employed to break into computers with an objective to strengthen the security.

"What if our choices differ?" Vinitha asked.

"The system automatically decides the best compromise based on multiple other factors including the interests of the nation." Vipul answered and attempted to change the topic as he was beginning to get uncomfortable.

"When is the appointment, Vinu?" he asked

"It is at 9.30 AM tomorrow."

"Listen. Tomorrow is Tuesday, from 3 PM to 4.30 PM it is *Rahu Kalam*[16] and from 9 AM to 10.30 AM *Yamakandam*[17]. Let us connect for the session before 9 AM. I don't want to start such an important phase in our life cycle in *Yamakandam*." Vipul exclaimed.

"Vipul, I cannot believe that you are worried about *Rahu Kalams* and *Yamakandams*. We are in the era of the science revolution. You are an IT professional. Come on!" Vinitha gently chided.

"Does not matter. Certain things will never change. My beliefs will never change. Culture and beliefs are not antitheses to science. Tradition will never die how much ever you progress in modern technology." Vipul was very passionate about culture and beliefs.

"Let us take an example. How much ever technology improves, a male cannot give birth to a child. Only women can beget, how

---

[16] Rahu Kalam & [17]Yamakandam -
Inauspicious periods of 90 minutes each in a day as per Hindu beliefs.

much ever women fight for their rights. That is God's creation." Vipul added.

"Who knows! That too can happen. Anyway, I know that it is a convenient argument for you male chauvinists. You take the name of God whenever it is convenient for you. It would be better if you can just understand better the sacrifices made by women and share their burden through just a little empathy which of course you would not do." Vinitha normally erupted in such discussions.

Vipul cursed himself for having started such a discussion. He had come to understand Vinitha well in his 3+ years of married life. Not surprisingly, it was Vinitha who came to his rescue immediately and kept the communication going.

"Anyway, science is changing even that. Don't you know that it is now possible to grow a child completely outside a woman's embryo for the entire nine months? Artificial embryo technology is possible today. An egg can be fertilized with semen outside an embryo and transferred safely to an artificial embryo where it can grow until released as a child. This is possible now and children born using this technology are found to be perfectly hale and healthy." Vipul thanked the advancement in science that saved him from an unpleasant argument.

"I am aware, but would you go in for an artificial embryo for your child?" Vipul countered.

"I might not."

"Why are we then talking about a technology which even a hard-core women's rights activist will not opt for? All technology advancements are not necessarily for the good of humankind."

"I don't agree. The artificial embryo is a boon to humankind. It is a God-sent opportunity for women suffering from infertility problems. Infertility is no longer a problem as long as healthy egg and semen are available. It is a boon. Probably, that is why the government brought in stupid controls for childbirth which I anyway believe is the RIGHT of a woman trampled upon."

"OK. OK. Leave that topic. Answer this. We can now order a new robot like our Sevugan complete with all six senses, in whatever colour, skin, capabilities, characteristics and it will get delivered at home within a week. Why are we still waiting to get the license for a biological child? How much ever effort you put in for designing your robot and how much ever money you pay, can a robot replace your child. It cannot. Would you ever be able to give your motherly love to a robot? Mother's love will never change despite any amount of science revolution. That is the reality we fail to understand." Vipul lectured.

"Cool, cool. OK. I will login by 8.45 AM. I don't want to get into another argument now. I want to get ready to go to my office. I need to submit an important *penetration test*[18] report today." Vinitha concluded the coffee session and walked towards the bathroom. Both remained excited and exuberant for the rest of

---

[18] Penetration test – Cyber security test conducted to identify the weaknesses in advance which could be exploited by hackers.

the day in anticipation of the much-awaited counselling session the next day.

| TUESDAY, 15ᵀᴴ APRIL 2121

Vipul and Vinitha were seated before the screen for the interview exactly by 8.50 for the 9.30 AM session, fearing the onset of *Yamakandam* at 9.00 AM. Adorned with headphones, touch gloves and thot-pad in their ears, fingers and forehead respectively. These are standard and mandatory accessories for all *shadverse*[1] collaboration meetings. All the six dimensions – speaker, microphone, 3D video, smell, touch and thought can be enabled or disabled as required.

They had been sufficiently briefed about the instructions to follow during multiple pre-counselling sessions. The briefing video was automatically pushed into and played on their phones for the last four days. It is a pre-condition that the briefing video

---

[1] shadverse – shad in India's classical language, Sanskrit means six. When the new technology of virtual collaboration using the six senses was invented in India, the inventor named it shadverse, indicative of six elements.

should have been viewed from the beginning to the end with a warning that the appointment would get automatically cancelled if the briefing video was stopped in between. Vipul and Vinitha did not know if there was an option to monitor them playing the video, but of course, they could not afford to miss the appointment and hence they had played the video in full, not once but twice to be sure.

Almost all government meetings happen in *shadverse* mode. *Shadverse* brings the closest to real-life experience that the virtual world could bring in – as of now. *Shadverse* enabled connecting people virtually using all the six senses known to humans – the latest technology added in the current decade to read 'communicated' thoughts using a thot-pad. Despite all this gadgetry, there were hardly any wires seen around. Except for the main charging point, all power and communications were through unseen communication channels. It was like an invisible tube that ran criss-cross across the room. These were marked by small light spots. Every room had these 'channels' for all new equipment, one had to just 'orient' them towards these channels. They automatically get 'linked'. This way the equipment could 'float' across the rooms seamlessly.

All meetings including judicial enquiry proceedings and search warrants nowadays happened in *shadverse*. Users must activate all the six channels in all the government meetings. People often tend to disable the 'thought mode' in meetings, especially in government meetings, to 'hide' their thoughts. Important government meetings like today's meeting automatically gets disconnected even if one channel is disabled. There were murmurs of protest on insisting on 'thought channel' in government meetings but the government was not bothered.

Their slot would automatically get cancelled if both of them were not signed in and taken their assessments before 9.20 AM, but Vipul and Vinitha had completed theirs much in advance. Video Verification Successful, the screen flashed and took them to the waiting room. Briefing videos were played in the waiting room again till the counsellor arrived.

"Good morning, Vipul and Vinitha." The counsellor's voice came clear and cheerful on the screen exactly at 9.30 AM. A man in big frame entered the screen with a big smile and a *namaste* to Vipul and Vinitha. Vipul did not fail to notice the picture of the Prime Minister Ashok Raj pinned to his shirt. He looked very confident and exuberant.

The cheerful voice immediately turned business-like. The government software must be a surprisingly advanced version. It must be having a voice modulator attached to the words that flashed on the teleprompter. Or it must be a recorded voice synced well with the face. One's expression cannot be so word-perfect.

"I must first confirm your voluntary acceptance. Can you please sign on the pads before you? Both of you need to sign your acceptance independently and visibly before the screen. We can proceed further only after this acceptance," the officer smiled.

Vipul and Vinitha digitally signed their acceptance using the touch pad in signature mode. The screen flashed 'Digital signature verified. Acceptance taken'. The screen came online again with the message, 'Debiting Rs. 70,000 from the primary account as the charge for this counselling session.' Again, a message. 'Please accept'. Both Vipul and Vinitha nodded their head as a token of acceptance. "Both of you are nodding your head. I need audio confirmation too. Please reply. Can I take it as acceptance?" the system asked again. Both Vipul and Vinitha shouted "Yes", afraid that if even one of their voices was not heard, they might be cut off from the line. It had become their – especially Vinitha's - lifeline now.

"I will have to make an obligatory announcement. Digital cigarettes are now banned during all government meetings. You cannot choose tobacco background for the smell. We have anyway automatically blocked this option in the settings for this meeting." He showed 'Smell virtual background' icon next to 'Video' and 'Audio' and 'Tobacco' in the pull-down menu which was shown as greyed out.

"I must now do some tests to confirm your readiness to welcome your progeny both physically as well as mentally. You will get your license only after the successful completion of these tests."

"Answer me, why do you want a child now? It is only three years and four months since your marriage. Your application is earlier than the average application time. The average period for Parenthood Application for this year is four years and seven months and the average for your city is four years and two months." The counsellor's voice sounded almost accusatory on the screen.

They had both agreed early on that Vipul will field most of the questions. He was less stressed about today's meeting and therefore less likely to 'react adversely'. "Both my grandparents died in a road accident last year and so we became eligible for a new addition to the family last year itself. I was very close to my grandfather and I long for a child in his memory. In fact, my gene composition choice is mostly like that of my grandfather's characteristics." Vipul replied.

The counsellor punched in a few commands in the system and satisfied himself that Vipul's statement was indeed true. He even pulled up the death record of his grandfather from the archives and shared it on the screen to get Vipul's confirmation that it was indeed that of his grandfather. There is a rule in 'Birth Control Act' that the total composition of a 'declared family' cannot exceed five and the definition for a 'declared family' is very complicated and not necessarily based on marriage or biology. Perhaps the only sure thing about it is that no one can be part of more than one 'declared family'.

The rules of 'caring' within the family were very strict. It was thought that violation of this would lead to a lot of penalty. So, one had to carefully choose one's 'family'.

Happily, though unintentionally, Vipul's grandfather, who was ailing, could get the benefits of 'family care' because he was part of Vipul's 'family'. And now, because of his passing away, Vipul could 'add' a new member to his 'family'.

"Now for the next question." The counsellor's voice broke into his reverie. "You don't have any support at home. How will you guarantee us that you will be able to give good care for your child?" The counsellor persisted.

They had prepared themselves for this question in advance. They even had a rehearsal between them. So, it was Vinitha's turn to answer. "My mother has agreed to stay with us for a year after the 'delivery' if the approval is sanctioned." Vinitha answered. She was also afraid that if both did not share the answers, it might be construed that they were not 'adequately interested'.

"Now for your choices. Both of you please independently choose your preferences on the attributes." The counsellor selected an option in the screen shared with Vipul & Vinitha and a form with 72 questions appeared on the wall screen including complexion, height, propensity to weight, hair colour, interest in sports, right brain dominance or left-brain dominance, memory capability, multi-tasking, learnability, analytical mind, rational thinking, temperament, etc. All the questions had detailed explanations and the choices in pulldown menus.

The counsellor took pains to explain the choices for all the 72 questions.

"I personally don't believe in my child getting tailor-made. But I understand that I don't have a choice." Vinitha grunted under her breath.

"Why now Vinu? We have already been briefed." Vipul protested in an equally low tone. He began to worry about Vinitha's expression now. Vinitha can be the most trusted partner if she was committed to a cause. But if she was not convinced, she would not easily cooperate. Vipul was more of a 'How-can-I-get-my things-done?' guy.

"It is OK Vipul. Allow her to express her feelings. We are used to this. We understand and appreciate your feelings, Vinitha. But the government of our country enacted a law, not this year, but five years back, making it mandatory for all the citizens to take prior approval to beget a child and that all children to be born in

India will mandatorily be a genetically improved child," the counsellor mediated.

"It is actually Genetically Modified child," Vinitha could not but express her opinion.

"You can use whatever term you want. We call this Mission GIC meaning Genetically Improved Child." Vipul wondered whether even the counsellor was getting frustrated with Vinitha's brutal honesty.

"It is OK. I know that I don't have a choice. Let us proceed," though not convinced Vinitha agreed.

"Actually, this is in fact giving the choice to you of how you want your child to be. Our objective is to make every parent's dream come true. Make all parents in India get the child of their wish. Advances in science in India make it possible. Enjoy this privilege. This has become a reality because of the tireless efforts of our Honourable Prime Minister Raj ji." The counsellor made a lengthy speech.

Vipul silently agreed with Vinitha's unspoken observation that it had become a practice for all the government officials to eulogize the Prime Minister at the first and of course every possible opportunity.

"But if you are not happy, you can stop this process any time. We will not compel you. We will in fact proceed with your application only after both of you approve." The counsellor gave a vicious smile, seemingly understood Vinitha's thoughts through the highly powerful thot-pad.

Vinitha could feel the viciousness in his smile even through the screen and said, "I understand, it is OK."

Though Vipul and Vinitha knew they had to make choices, they had not got the list of options in advance. The options differed from parent to parent to prevent stereotyping. So, there was no 'predictability' and therefore no way they could have discussed and agreed beforehand. Vipul and Vinitha could only hope that they gave 'matching' responses to most of the questions. While broadly they had agreed on choices like complexion, eye colour and all that, they had never discussed about the cognitive and affective choices. The truth was that they had cause to worry. Both Vipul and Vinitha were considered an 'ideal couple'. But they were completely different personalities. May be that is why they were well-matched, but their preferences on political, social and economic issues were almost diametrically opposite. Their skills differed, but their interests matched. Their physical qualities were different, but they were both conscientious and socially concerned. Their life attitudes varied, but life goals matched. They were good for each other but had to have their 'spaces'.

Still, to both, it was a big surprise that many questions were more on intellectual and emotional factors, and both were not prepared for it. They were not given the option of discussing during the meeting though they were in the same room as the government wanted the choices to be natural and instinctive. Vinitha had a sneaky feeling that the system had known about their 'differences' and had specifically designed such a 'questionnaire'. Vipul, of course, was worried that Vinitha would demonstrate her independence in her choices and was worried that they may end up losing the 'opportunity'.

Vipul pressed SUBMIT button first, followed by Vinitha who took five more minutes to complete the form.

"We could crack gene sequencing only for 72 factors and there are lots more for which scientists don't have a clue yet. But our Honourable Prime Minister is very confident that we will crack all the gene factors before the end of this decade. We keep improving and a day will come when we can copy and replicate human's genetic sequence like taking a photocopy or even a 3D print. Our scientists are working very hard on this mission and India is leading the world in this research. Wait and watch, India will be the first to come out with 'human gene designing' technology. Our Honourable Prime Minister will make this happen before the end of his term for sure," the counsellor was apparently well trained and would never forget to add the prefix 'honourable' before every mention of the prime minister.

Vinitha thought to herself, "How does it matter to my longing for a child? Please come to the point."

"The Prime Minister is not a scientist. How can he take credit for such a discovery? If and probably, when India manages to crack this first, it will be to the credit of the scientists." Vinitha thought to herself but quickly changed her thought. She restrained herself with great difficulty not to express or show any emotion. It was so 'unVinitha-like' But being an IT expert herself, that too specialising in cyber security, she knew that all government meetings get recorded automatically and an automated speech analysis engine scans through all the recordings to identify and alert objectionable discussions. These engines did not just analyse semantics, they were so advanced, that they could analyse the modulation, tone, amplitude and even frequency, to understand the underlying emotion and feelings. There is a separate wing in the CBI which goes through tons of recordings for the so-called objectionable content. Everyone knows that expressing views contrary to the opinion of the government is given the name 'sedition' and if serious, could land a person in jail.

"But I don't understand how you would fix things like complexion. Does not sound rational." Vipul could make his question sound more curious than doubtful. He was adept at it.

"You have a very fair complexion. How did you get such a good complexion?" the counsellor asked. Vinitha was seething inside. These men. Centuries can go by. But their fascination for fair skin will never diminish.

"Both my parents are fair, and my mother told me that she was given *kungamapoo*[2] by her mother when she was carrying me," Vipul announced proudly.

---

[2] kungamapoo – Saffron, it is a common belief that when a woman carrying a child consumes saffron, the child is likely to get a fair complexion.

"You believe that eating *kungamapoo*[2] can change the complexion of the baby, but you don't want to believe that correcting the gene can change the complexion of the baby," the counsellor laughed. Vipul managed to look sheepish. Vinitha wanted to answer that it was not the possibility or impossibility of it but the ethical aspect of it that *got her goat*. She always rose to defend Vipul even though Vipul could do it himself. She just chose to exercise restraint in this aspect. Restraint was possibly the better defence here.

"Anyway, there is only a 68% correlation between your choices. Why so much difference between both of you?" the counsellor's voice intervened.

"Possibly because my grandfather is my role model and her mother for her. Maybe we could not come to an agreement on certain traits," Vipul clarified. He continued. 'That even shows that our choices are genuine." That was smart of him. The counsellor sounded impressed.

"The average correlation on child trait selection we find in our country is 76% based on last year's data. You are slightly below that, but your correlation is more than the minimum requirement which is 60%, Hence your choices can be considered but only if you accept the lower correlation score. In case both of you want to discuss this some more and come to a greater agreement, we will give you some more time and do the test again. Maybe your scores will improve. Do you want to go ahead with this score, or would you want to try again for a greater agreement? Both of you need to agree on this decision. Even if one of you disagrees, you need to take the test again. This is a very important step. You can take your time to decide. You will now see your choice and your spouse's choice side by side in your individual screens," the counsellor pressed a button to open the screens for them.

This was one decision they were both sure they would agree upon. Both were never interested in the test in the first place. Vinitha, because she wanted a childbirth as natural as possible, and the joy of surprises while bringing up the child and Vipul, because he simply didn't want any more tests.

For the sake of procedure, Vipul and Vinitha chatted for a while and pressed the ACCEPT button.

After the counsellor gave his confirmation, the system prompted "FINAL GENE MATCHING PATTERN READY" and displayed the correlated choices as the third column in the display next to Vipul's and Vinita's choices. Vinitha did not even want to see the final choice. That somebody else – somebody who doesn't even know them as a person finalising the most important decision of their life was somehow unacceptable to her. Given a choice, she would have gone to a forest and given birth to a baby amidst nature. But she didn't have the luxury of choice.

The counsellor's voice came again, "Your application is approved, and you get a license that will be valid for two years from today. Your gene report is ready and copied to your medical record in an encrypted format. You can share this report with your reproduction consultant so that he or she can match and start the gene treatment for you. You would already be aware that this is required to be done before you stop your birth control medication. And one last important warning. You can choose your choice of gene pattern, but gender selection is not legal. That is why we did not include gender in any of the 72 factors given for choice. Don't try any illegal gender selection attempt."

"What is the probability of getting a child of our preference?" Vinitha asked.

"Please remember that your correlation is only 68%. As per the AI/ML[3] analysis, for this correlation and pattern, the cumulative probability of matching to the correlated list is 65%. Remember the correlated list and not your individual lists," the counsellor answered.

"Can we close the session with this? Don't forget to fill-up the feedback form about this session before you sign off. Remember, it is thanks to our Honourable Prime Minister that we are able to bring you this technology for the first time in the world." The counsellor wished them and extended his hand from the screen. Vipul adorned his touchpad in his palm and gave the hand movement equivalent of a handshake. Vinitha followed suit. Both felt the firm handshake typical of a counsellor. Vipul and Vinitha could even feel the hardness of his hand.

"OK. I must give this message to you before we end the session. Virologists have confirmed that the reported incidents of the mysterious illness are found to be from a virus. This virus

---

[3] AI / ML – Aritificial Intelligence / Machine Learning

transmits from human to human and is highly infectious. World Wellness Organisation, (WWO) named the virus, Covid2121 on the lines of a virus which shook the world from 2019 to 2022. Be on your guard. Don't go out unless it is an emergency. Get prepared to face a lockdown. All the best," and the counsellor's image walked inside the screen.

"What are the chances of getting the child of our choice? Is it practical?" Vinitha asked Vipul.

"Same probability as the chances of one of us getting infected by Covid2121." Vipul could not take his thoughts out of Covid2121.

"I am very sceptical," said Vinitha.

"Why are you sceptical? I know that your father believes in astrology as I see all your family horoscopes in your digital container. When you can believe that a horoscope could determine the characteristics of a person, why cannot you believe that genes can determine the characteristics of a person?" Vipul exclaimed.

"You are mistaken on two counts. One, horoscopes don't determine a person's characteristics. They explain them, which is like your test report giving the figures. They don't make the figures. They help you understand the symptoms. Horoscopes are just reports." She took a few seconds' deep breath. "Second, I never underestimated the power of science. I know the power of genes and that genes do determine the characteristics of a child. I believe that a horoscope could spell out the characteristics of a person, but horoscopes don't modify a person's character. You can't even modify them. It is not possible to tailor-make a horoscope. Horoscopes just report the creator's choice to us. You can pray or do alternatives to mediate the impact. Similarly, I am not able to agree that it is possible to stereotype genes to one's choice. It is the job of the Creator and humans should not usurp that role. Life expectancy has increased in the last 50 years, but science can never achieve freedom from death. It is against the nature of law." Vinitha explained.

"What if the child has some ailments? It is to avoid such contingency that all this gene engineering has arisen." Vipul persisted.

"Why are you so pessimistic? 'Gene correction' was not in practice when we were born. Have we not turned out alright?" Vinitha's argument had no answer. Vipul realised that he needed to change the direction of the conversation.

"Do you know that 'gene correction' technology figures in our great epic *Mahabharat*[4] as well?" Vipul smiled.

"*Mahabharat!* Where in *Mahabharat*?"

"Kunti got her four children exactly of her choice, with all the characteristics she liked. How was that possible if not 'gene correction'? Not only she got sons of her choice, she taught the technology of 'gene correction' to Madri as well," Vipul smiled. Vipul was very fond of classical literature, and he quoted from literature quite often.

---

[4] Mahabharat – One of the two Hindu epics, the other being Ramayana.

"That is not 'gene correction'. That is courtesy the power of a *mantra* given by Rishi Durvasa pleased by Kunti's caregiving." Vinitha explained.

"'The *Mahabharat* says by the power of a *mantra*. Our science says by the power of science. At the end of the day, the result is the same. Simple. So, the power of 'genetic engineering' is not new to us Indians. We knew it in the last *yuga* itself," Vipul laughed.

"Science has already proved that it is possible to custom modify the genes. Let us just put all these behind us. We just now completed the organized formal session. Leave it at that. We are going to get a child of our choice in another ten months. Let us look forward to that." Vipul smiled.

"At the moment, I don't mind if science wins over nature, though I think it can never do. Nature will find a way to assert itself. I would be happy if I get our child, of our choice or not, is irrelevant. I am waiting for my child, ideal or not, and I am happy that a beginning has been made today." Vinitha also changed over to the positive side of things.

"I checked the form thoroughly, but there was no mention of health or life expectancy in the form." Vinitha said. "Health is what the government should focus on. Not designing a child but keeping it healthy whatever its personality be."

"Science can never achieve immortality. Creation, Protection and Destruction are the privileges of our Creator. I would be happy as long as my child is healthy and happy. Other things don't matter much to me though I have given some preference or the other. Let us see how it goes." Vipul closed the discussion.

Sevugan came and said, "*Vanakkam. Enna vendum inraiya dinnerku*[5]. Shall I prepare a dish you would love? It is called *kuzhi paniyaram*. You cannot get this in any of the hotels. I learnt the recipe from an old video on tubevideo. Do you want to try?"

"What is this *kuzhipaniyaram*? I know that *kuzhi* in Tamil means a hole. Is it the *vada* we prepare with a hole in it?" Vinitha asked. Vipul explained, "Sevugan is learning Tamil to speak to us more naturally. It seems that he has caught a fancy towards everything Tamil. Tamil heritage food as well. Soon Sevugan may even start writing Tamil poetry. What Sevugan?"

"True and false. I am learning Tamil, out of my passion for the language, not just for the sake of speaking to you. I can speak to you in English as well." Sevugan clarified.

"It is OK. One and the same. Stop nit-picking." Vinitha said.

"I have in fact, written my first Tamil poetry motivated by Bharathiar's poetical skills. Do you want to hear my first Tamil poem?" asked Sevugan looking at both of them with the expectations of a child.

"Go ahead," Vinitha responded unenthusiastically.

"I will not recite to an audience who is not interested in my skills." Sevugan replied and went back.

---

[5] In tamil meaning "What do you want for dinner tonight?"

After ensuring that Sevugan was not anywhere near, Vinitha asked Vipul to come closer and said in a hushed tone, "I am finding Sevugan's behaviour often very odd especially nowadays. We have to watch carefully. Otherwise, he could turn defiant. Already my friends tell me that we do not control him adequately."

"Don't worry. Sevugan is good. Managing a 'Next Generation Robot' is not an easy task. We need to reorient ourselves a lot and adjust a lot to them. If we want Next Gen Services, we need to adjust to Next Gen behaviour. It is more complex than even leadership skills. I went through a special training program on managing next generation robots, so I know something about it. It is very complex."

"It doesn't look like your course has done much good for you, I mean your robot management training course. I feel Sevugan is turning rebellious. If you leave him like this, he could become a 'troublemaker'."

"I will fine-tune his 'deep learning index'. Currently, I have left it at the highest score, i.e., 99.99. It is adventurous and fun to work with a robot with 99.99 'deep learning index' and I want to experience the extent of his learning ability. If he is good, he can personally teach our child too. Of course, 'high learning index' poses a risk as well. Uncontrolled learning at times can increase the 'defiance index' automatically and unknowingly. It is like bringing up a teenage child. It is a big risk if the 'defiance index' of 'next generation robot' goes above 50%. We need to monitor him on a daily basis and fine-tune his 'deep learning index'. Don't worry. I am monitoring his indices daily. His 'defiance index' is still hovering around safe 20 to 30% only." Vipul assured her.

"How can you compare managing a robot to that of rearing a child? Managing is different from rearing. You said earlier that a robot can never replace a biological child. You seem to be contradicting your own statement." Vinitha countered Vipul.

"A robot cannot replace a child. I am clear about it. But managing a robot is almost similar to that of managing a teenage child. This is the first lesson in our 'Robot management training.'" Vipul tried to explain but Vinitha was not convinced.

"Of course, there is one big difference. I can see the metrics in a robot clearly and adjust accordingly whereas it is not that easy to see the metrics in a teenage child." Vipul added quickly.

"I don't know if you are monitoring or not. He is becoming more and more defiant. If at 20-30%, he is so strong-willed, I dread to think of him at 50. Forget about 70-80. Reduce his 'deep learning index' today itself. It is OK if he does not learn. I want an obedient robot rather than an intelligent learning robot. When will the change come into effect?"

"Don't raise your voice. Remember, Sevugan's hearing power is five times that of us, humans. He can hear voices clearly even from the garden. He can hear even when he is sleeping." Vipul reminded

"Would he then hear our conversations in the bedroom?" Vinitha asked with serious concern.

"Don't worry my beautiful and always cautious wife. I have installed jammers in the bedrooms so that robots cannot hear our bedroom secrets. My learning index is very high, you know." Vipul smiled.

"But he hears whatever you sing in the bathroom. He told me last week that you sing very well." Vipul quickly added.

Vinitha gave an expression that she did not appreciate the pun. "Don't entertain such talks with him. Let us install jammers in the bathrooms as well." Vinitha raised her voice.

"Leave your worries about Sevugan to me. I will take care of him. He is not rebellious. Being young, his curiosity is very high, and it looks like rebellion to you. I will reduce his 'learning index'. The change will apply from tonight 8 PM." Vipul assured her and left. He did not want to continue the discussion further.

"I don't know what you will do. Let us not spoil him by being too kind. My grandmother used to quote often, '*Spare the rod and spoil the child*'." Vinitha murmured.

"Sevugan is not a child and there is no option to use a rod on Sevugan. You will end up spoiling his electronics or breaking the rod."

"OK. Enough of your Sevugan affection. Let us check if there is any update about the virus. The whole of India is in fear of this virus. Forget about your stupid robot." Vinitha snubbed Vipul and asked *Abra* to show 'Hot News'.

"Robogenius, the largest robot company in the world, announced today that they are withdrawing their latest patch[6] update version 7.4.1. The CEO of Robogenius, Vinod Sharma, said in a news conference today that the decision to withdraw the new version was taken as a few critical bugs have been reported in 7.4.1 version of the OS. This version is applicable only for the home edition of Next Generation Robots. He requested all NGN robot users to check their patch level and downgrade to 7.4.0 which is a stable version if using 7.4.1. He expressed regret for the slip," the newsreader announced.

Then the news started flashing the video instructions for checking the patch level in the robot and the procedure to downgrade the patch level.

"Vipul, I am aware that Sevugan is from Robogenius. Please check which patch version we are using currently." Vinitha said or rather ordered.

"I know for sure we are using 7.4.0 only. Not to worry. I always disable auto patch updates and use one version lower. I know buggy patches do come and I never upgrade to the current patch version immediately. I update to the last known version whenever they update to a new version. That way, I never had to face issues from buggy patches. I always use a stable patch version only."

---

[6] patch – Update in software code usually released to address reported security issues and/or bugs.

"That is not necessarily a good practice, Vipul. It sounds good but very risky. New patches do fix many known vulnerabilities in the previous version. We, cyber security experts, create awareness about the risks arising from using old patches and encourage everyone to update to the latest patch quickly. If not patched, attackers might exploit known vulnerabilities. It is an irony that my own husband is not aware and my own robot is not patched. What Vipul?"

"That is OK. That is the cyber security perspective. As a user, I know the challenges of using just released patches like what you heard in the news just now."

"I need to understand the background about patch 7.4.1 and analyse the reported bugs before I can comment on your statement. I will remember to do it anyway out of my curiosity. But it is not a good idea not to patch, you may end up with more complex problems. It is interesting that there are two unconnected, but very strange incidents that happened in two days. Both the incidents happen very rarely, probably once in a century but here they happened on two consecutive days."

Vipul was not interested to change his opinion about robotics. He believed strongly that he was the robotics expert like Vinitha was the cyber security expert. He strongly believed that Vinitha should not interfere in his domain as he never interfered in her cyber security matters.

| WEDNESDAY, 16TH APRIL 2121

Vinitha opened her Inbox on the phone in the morning only to see a red flag message with sombre background music waiting for her. Sombre music starts playing as soon as a serious message with a possible bad news gets selected. Vinitha realized that the message was of high priority and something must be wrong, and began panicking. Flags and mood get automatically updated based on the content of the message. This new feature helps phone users to gauge the intent and content of the message before opening the message. Vinitha got up late because of the emotional stress from the previous day's counselling session and put her phone on 'chup chaap' mode and hence missed a couple of high priority calls from her mother.

Now when she was having coffee and reading her messages, this red flag message made her guilty and anxious. Vipul could sense her anxiety. "Why are you getting tense without even reading the message? Read the message first." Vipul advised.

"Because it is from my mother. I dread receiving sombre mood message from amma." Vinitha explained.

Vinitha opened the message and her mother's voice came on the speakers and her tearful face came on the screen.

"Vinu, appa had a heart attack in the morning, and we are rushing him to the hospital now. I tried to reach you a couple of times, but your presence was showing 'chup chaap' mode. Our next-door neighbour is helping me. I am very worried, kanna." Her mother's voice sounded tired and vanished from the screen.

"Call her back. Let us understand the situation. If required, we must get ready to leave." Vipul comforted her. Vinitha's parents were staying alone in their family home near Madurai. Vinitha had been asking them to move to Chennai to stay with them for some time, but they would not listen. They were not interested to move out of their ancestral home in Madurai.

"She will not be at home. She must be on the way to the hospital or could be at the hospital." Vinitha said.

"How does it matter? You can call her UDIC[1] and the call will automatically find the best possible device to connect. Very

---

[1] UDIC – Unique Digital Identification Code. Each citizen gets a unique UDIC registered for them at the time of birth. All their contact coordinates including their home phone, office phone, hand phone, email ID, shadverse ID are automatically connected to the UDIC and seamlessly connected to an available channel. This is known as SDIE (Seamless Digital Interaction Experience)

convenient. We no longer need to remember multiple complex numbers. The calls will automatically go to her hand phone if she is not at home." Vinitha knew this was true. She was normally not so helpless. But her mother's voice had upset her deeply.

Most of the developing countries have already moved to UDIC calling. All the telecom service providers in India had already implemented 'Personal call interface' protocol whereby the individual's UDIC gets linked to the telecom presence of any individual. It is no longer necessary to remember or even record multiple phone numbers or user IDs, email IDs and calling codes. UDIC gets mapped to the individual's digital presence if the individual is present online or through the offline network to the individual's phone network if not online. One has to just link the UDIC with the contact's name. Since UDIC is a 25-character code, it is easily recognisable. The network automatically tracks the individual's location and intelligently routes the call to the best possible media presence of the individual. All the calls start with 5D calls and switch from there up to a single dimension which is audio only, depending on the availability of sense modes.

Vinitha's call got routed to the hand phone of her mother as her phone was identified to be 'not at home.' Her GPS location was tagged on to her UDIC ID. The call would first go to the home system if the hand phone was identified to be 'at home' using its mapped GPS location. That call went to her hand phone. She answered the call, and her video and audio came live on Vinitha's wall screen.

Vinitha could see her mother, Vijaya, in a hospital room sitting next to a bed. Her father was lying on the bed and it was visible that something was amiss. Vijaya was sobbing. "appa had a mild heart attack this morning, Vinu."

Vinitha asked, "What did the doctor say?"

"I did not understand fully. I am too tense. Anyway, you can hear it yourself." Vijaya paired her phone to the system at the bedside and pressed the 'Announce' button on the bedside system.

Vinitha listened to the status message left by the doctor. Vinitha then asked the system to answer her anxious questions including the discharge time, discharge instructions, expected payment at the time of discharge, etc. The system gave her a long lesson as to the cause of his heart attack and the precautions to be taken post-discharge and the probability of getting a heart attack again if they did not follow the physician's instructions.

"Did you get all the necessary information from the BOT? Do we need to call the doctor?" Vipul asked.

"I got all the information including his diet requirement, medication, next consultation date, etc. I don't think we need to call the doctor. He is getting discharged this afternoon. They don't keep patients longer than absolutely needed in the hospital as most treatments are now possible at home. If required, the hospital will send a trained nurse robot to the house. It appears that the critical stage is behind us. We may not have much to worry for now. There is one question not answered though, if he is in a fit position to travel to Chennai."

"What did the BOT say for that question?" Vipul was curious.

"Usual. 'I am sorry that I cannot help you on this. I am not finding any information tagged as travel in his case history. You must ask the physician. I will remind the physician to include travel advisory from the next case'." Vinitha mimicked the robot's voice. "Shall I see if the physician is available to talk to you?" and the MEDBOT came online after some time and said, "Sorry, your physician is performing a surgery and hence not in a position to answer you."

"I got you. It is worth going all the way to Madurai and bringing them back with us. How do we know if he is fit to travel?" Vipul asked.

"I have registered the question; I got a message that the reply to my query will reach my Inbox in about two hours." Vinitha replied.

Her mother came back on the line. "What did you understand Vinu? I am very worried."

"Don't worry amma. The attack is not severe. He will be discharged this afternoon. Nothing to worry if the medication is taken regularly. He will not even require a robot nurse. We are anyway coming over now. Don't worry." Vinitha comforted her.

"Your pain balm smell is sickening, amma. Is it from you or from appa?" Vinitha asked.

"You know I get a severe headache when I am tense. I cannot help it." amma replied defensively. She was as much in awe of her daughter as she chastised her. Their bond was very strong.

"Your balm is too strong, and you have the bad habit of applying almost a whole bottle of balm on your forehead. The smell repels us even through a phone call. I can imagine how strong it would be there." Vinitha blew her nose. "Take care amma. Let me get ready to come over there."

"One minute Vinu. I have this offering with me, and I need to somehow send this to *Ezhumalayan*[2]." Vijaya showed her a yellow cloth tied in a knot.

"What is this amma? What has this to do with appa's health?" Vinitha wanted to get ready to leave at the earliest.

"I remembered to take a 50 Rupee coin and tie it in a yellow cloth to offer to Tirupati Balaji before the ambulance came. I am keeping it safe with me. See, appa will come home without even a scar because of the grace of *Ezhumalayan*[2]."

"amma, You will never change. We are in the era of robotics and you are still practicing your '*manja thuni kanikkai*[3]'. Nuisance though it is, that is sweet of you. Don't worry. We will figure out a way to reach it to your *Ezhumalayan*." Vinitha finished the discussion and disconnected the call. She cleared the hospital payment online.

"My mother has been asking me to visit her for a long time. Let us visit them today before the possible dreadful lockdown. My father looks sick. Let us try and bring them to Chennai with us. I don't want them to suffer alone during the lockdown. We don't know how long the lockdown will continue. I was told that it could continue for six months. We can go today and try to return tonight itself." Vinitha spurted out.

---

[2] Ezhumalayan – Other name for Lord Balaji, Lord of seven hills.
[3] manja thuni kanikkai – Practice of tying an offering to God in a yellow cloth at the time of a crisis.

Vipul was not interested in travelling, especially after hearing the news about the virus but could not refuse her. It was a fair request from the only child of an unwell father.

"OK. Let us take the Emery. It is more convenient for long distance. It will take about 2.5 hours in all to reach Madurai."

"Give me an hour to get ready. I don't want to depend on outside food. We cannot take any chance now. I will prepare some idlis and podi quickly for us. I am not sure if amma would be in a fit mental state to prepare food." Vinitha offered. Vipul moved to his study room to finish pending office work.

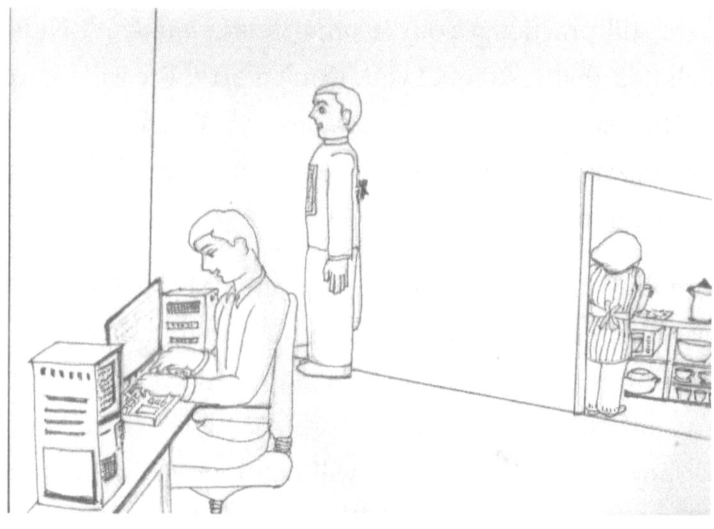

When Vipul was in the middle of his office work, Vinitha came out of the kitchen shouting, "I received the reply message in my Inbox – doctor gave the clearance to bring appa to Chennai. We are leaving. No escape now." She announced and went right back in. That was Vinitha. She had to act, immediately. She had also sensed Vipul's teeny-weeny hesitation. But she had to go. If she had nothing to do, she would fret. She had to do something. She was a born solution-finder. She preferred cyber security practice possibly because of the challenges, thrills and daily learnings her job brings. If there was a problem, she would set out to find a solution, like a sniffer dog, tenacious till she resolved it. Vipul loved that part of her though worried that she got into trouble often because of that trait.

While Vinitha was packing the idlis in a battery-operated packet which would keep the idlis fresh and hot for minimum 12 hours, Vipul locked the doors and gave instructions to Sevugan. He loaded the list of tasks to be completed and instructed the robot to take care of the safety of the house and not to venture out, until they returned.

"When are you likely to get back?" Sevugan asked in his deep voice.

"Tonight, or tomorrow." Vipul replied.

"Why don't you give one answer? You humans confuse us often. Learn from us robots. We always give a clear answer. If there is a doubt, we qualify our answers very clearly with the probability of that happening. You should tell me that the probability of returning tonight is 65% and 35% for tomorrow morning." Sevugan advised in a serious tone.

"OK sir. Understood. Will follow next time." Vipul teased the robot.

"Can I watch the IPL final match today on the TV when you are away? " IPL is the popular *flocric* tournament and *flocric* is a religion in India. The game of cricket improved over the years using digital technologies. Players wear special digital shoes and can fly short distances to catch the ball while it is in the air. They can control the direction and speed of their flight using small buttons in their hands. Smart flyers are very useful to a team to get the opposition players out quickly and they get auctioned for a large sum. The bowlers are allowed to vary their line and length, using the pace from their digital shoes, without running long distances. The batsmen wear a digital glass which gives them advance predictions on possible line, length, pace, swing, etc. The predictions turn out to be only 65% accurate though. Bowlers change the variety for every ball to beat the machine learning capability of the batsmen's system. Only systems approved and provided by the board can be used though.

"OK, only when we are away." Vipul was very clear this time.

"With your permission, I have recorded your statement so that you don't blame me in the Robot Court later." Sevugan said with a serious note.

"I don't want to miss today's match. Uday Naik is a sensational bowler and he is playing today. He has perfected a new type of delivery called 'juggly' which deceives even the computer. The computer gets confused and gives wrong predictions to the batsman. In the last match the batsman removed the computer glass when Uday Naik bowled." The house robot justified its request.

"OK Sevugan but remember to charge yourself before it goes below 20%. Don't forget in the excitement of 'juggly'. Else you will lie dead until we return. Also, remember, you need to synch your instructions by 8 PM and you have to be in the front room for the synch to be successful." Vipul gave a series of instructions

"Vipul, remember to load the instruction to water the garden plants. Sevugan conveniently forgets to water the plants." Vinitha came out of the kitchen with the idli packets ready in hand.

"Madam does not like me. She always complains." Sevugan said with a mischievous smile.

"No worries. I will load the instructions." Vipul replied and avoided further discussion.

The Emery is a small flyomative, comfortable for a small family of four to five members. It comes in self-driven model, auto pilot option & driverless option. Vipul did not go in for driverless option. He enjoyed driving and hence did not want to spend

additionally on the driverless model. The Emery can also be used for driving on roads, but it is not that effective on the roads. The Emery can fly at a maximum height of 40 meters from the ground level. With the shortest clearance for take-off and landing; it can take-off from a house terrace as well. They didn't use the Emery for daily travel on the road.

Vipul and Vinitha took the lift to the terrace where their flyo parking slot was located. Emery took off directly from the terrace but landed immediately on the entry road to their house. Flyos are not allowed to fly inside city roads and streets. Vipul noticed the time as 2.50 PM when they took off from the terrace. Vipul had to drive on the road until they reached the airway entrance. Flyos can use the aerial route only along identified airways which stop at the periphery of a city. There are a few limited airways called interconnects that criss-cross Chennai city primarily to connect to the long-distance airways. These are used for travel within the city but one would still need to use the roads until one reached the nearest airway or inter connect. This was to avoid the airway accidents as flyos need to safely negotiate through several high-rise buildings. Many buildings were higher than flyo's permitted flying height.

Airways are built avoiding the descent and take-off paths of commercial flights. Commercial airlines fly typically at higher altitudes ranging from 100 to 200 meters and they need to avoid crossing airways during their take-off and descent. Vipul chose a safe height of 30 meters after crossing Chennai limits. The transport department had identified aerial routes between the cities and had established towers on the routes for guiding flyos safely along the airways. Deviating from the designated airways is considered risky though possible as the flyos might face high-rise buildings on the path. Airways are surveyed, numbered and tagged so that the identified airways are free of high-rise buildings. High-rise buildings are not permitted along the airways.

Multiple airways are available between Chennai and Madurai with connecting cords between the different airways so that the passengers can switch between the airways when there is high traffic in one airway. Information about the traffic pattern in the airways got displayed at the airway entrance. Vipul chose the shortest airway between Chennai and Madurai which usually gets crowded. Vipul did not see much traffic on the airway and hence was able to drive easily at a speed of 350 kms per hour.

Vipul touched down at the Madurai Airway exit by 4.55 PM. Vipul was concerned if it would be peak traffic time in Madurai and it proved to be so. Traffic on Madurai roads was very high probably because everyone wanted to leave or return, considering the imminent lockdown. It was almost 6.05 PM by the time the emery could enter the gates of his father-in-law's house, an independent house on the outskirts of Madurai which was inherited by his father-in-law.

It was over six months since Vipul had last met his in-laws. Though it took only two to three hours to travel from Chennai to Madurai, Vipul and Vinitha had not travelled much. Vinitha made it a point to talk to her parents daily on 5D mode.

Vinitha's father, Varad and mother Vijaya were very fond of Vinitha as well as Vipul. Vinitha was their only child and hence they were very close to each other. Vipul lost his father at a young age and hence treated Varad as his own father. He affectionately called him Varadappa at times, meaning 'Father Varad'.

Varad used to say, "The original name given to me by my father is Varadappan and I shortened it to Varad as everyone in my office except me had short names. My father insisted on calling me Varadappa until he breathed his last." He instinctively liked Vipul calling him Varadappa.

Varad was at home and was sitting on the swing in the veranda. Vipul enjoyed the swing every time he visited his in-laws. One cannot afford to have a big house to accommodate swings in Chennai. Such small pleasures are possible in small towns or on the outskirts of big cities only. Vinitha's parents were very happy to see them.

Vipul and Vinitha updated them on the happy news of the approval for an imminent new entrant into the family. Vinitha asked them to pack to leave quickly.

Vinitha's parents agreed to come with them to Chennai but suggested that they stay back for the night and leave in the morning, after breakfast. Vijaya was worried about traveling in the night with a sick husband. But Vipul insisted on leaving right away after dinner, as he was worried about the imminent lockdown.

"Let us not take any chance but leave right away. Because the evening news mentioned about increasing deaths from the virus and that the lockdown could be announced any time. Once it is announced, they would deactivate the airway, the airway signals would be lost, whereby they couldn't guide the emery in the air. We would be forced to drive by road which would be even more painful. It is OK to drive in the night so that we reach Chennai before midnight."

It was 9.30 PM when they took off from the airway entrance and an alert sound came from the car radio before they reached the airway toll booth. Red alert sound comes automatically whenever there is an important announcement from the government on a separate frequency for its communication; this message would get activated automatically, without the need to tune to that frequency. If the radio device is powered on and even if it is playing on any other channel, it would switch automatically to this priority channel. The radio announced: "Standby for an important announcement from the Honourable Prime Minister of India," and automatically got connected to the Prime Minister's channel with the PM's image and voice, on the car dashboard screen.

"*Namaskar deshvasiyon.* This is your *pyare* Prime Minister speaking on an important announcement for you. We are in a difficult situation, based on the information I receive from my counterparts across the world. I need all your support to steer the country from a serious difficulty. With a heavy heart, I am announcing complete lockdown from today midnight, for the next ten days, to contain the dreaded contagious virus Covid2121. Our forefathers had faced a similar problem a hundred years back and a lockdown helped at that time. India acted responsibly and sensibly at that time also and remained a beacon of hope for the entire world, during that pandemic. I am confident that we will come out of this predicament as well, successfully....". The Prime Minister went on to explain the details, for ten more minutes. It is impossible to switch off the messages from the PM. A message would automatically go to the Ministry of I&B who are empowered to take action, if anyone ignores the Prime Minister's message knowingly, under the National Security and Safety Act.

The Prime Minister quoted a verse from the *Ramayan*[4] and Vipul reduced the volume and kept the video and audio ON until the Prime Minister completed his speech.

"Our Prime Minister makes important announcements, always from the midnight of the same day." Varad commented. Vipul could not guess, if it was a sarcastic remark or an appreciation.

"At last, he has announced. I expected yesterday itself" Vipul said.

Though they planned to reach well before midnight, they were delayed. They reached the outskirts of Chennai close to midnight. Though the lockdown was supposed to start only after midnight, Vipul's flyo was brought down repeatedly, at multiple places, by the AirWay Traffic Wing, to check the justification for travel and their identification. It involved a lot of extra time to come down

---

[4] Ramayan – Ramayan and Mahabharat are the two Hindu epics.

and take-off every time. The airway signals were switched off exactly at midnight and Vipul had no option but to bring down the Emery near Singaperumalkoil and drive on the road for the rest of the journey.

They reached home by 00.45 AM. Vinitha pressed the video doorbell, but none came to open the door. There was no indication of any activity inside. After waiting for five minutes, Vipul decided to use his override to open the door. Vipul showed his face to the door and said, "*Abra*, open the door, key to open 'mysweethome123'" a voice came back "Override request accepted, video authentication and key matched. But please change your key immediately as the password is simple to guess. If not changed in the next one hour, your key will be deactivated." The door opened but *Abra* ridiculed them with a heckle.

When Vinitha was making all the arrangements for her parents to sleep in the guest room, Vipul looked for Sevugan but could not find him anywhere in the house. There was a direct communication channel between Vipul's watch and Sevugan. Vipul activated the channel, but Sevugan could not be traced. It could happen only if Sevugan missed his battery charge or if he had gone out of the coverage area. Where could he have gone when Vipul specifically instructed him not to go out of the house until they returned? Was Sevugan turning rebellious? Would he come back or not? Vipul started wondering how to trace a missing robot. There should be many video guides in tubevideo for tips on tracing a missing robot, but he had no energy to search for the videos after a long day.

Vipul had to make a complaint with Robo Cop Force but again was very tired to make any effort that night. He decided to take it up the next day and went to bed.

THURSDAY, 17TH APRIL 2121

Vipul snoozed *Abra* alarm the next day thrice and that made his disciplinary score to go further down. Vipul finally got up hearing the voice of Sevugan. Sevugan's voice could not be snoozed. Vipul went down and was very angry seeing Sevugan talking in an excited voice.

"I apologize for disobeying your instructions, but it was unavoidable. One of our fellow robot committed suicide by short-circuiting and blasting himself at Adayar, apparently due to excessive harassment by his owner. You know, I am the President of the Robots Welfare Association of Nungambakkam. I could not avoid going to the enquiry. We made a representation to the National Robot Rights Commission and they promised us appropriate action against the owner."

"What are your demands?" Vipul wanted to know genuinely. He was always interested in robot welfare and considered himself a champion of robot rights.

"We are asking for stricter penalties to humans who abuse robots as robot suicides are increasing. We are proposing worktime restrictions for robots. Robots should not be made to work for more than ten hours in a day. There are labour law clauses covering maximum work hours and minimum wages for humans, but we don't have any such protection." Sevugan explained.

"Interesting. I heard some news that the government is proposing to bring a constitutional amendment to enact a Robot Protection Act with many such protections to robots in this parliament session itself. The only challenge is that some influential industrialists are opposing the Act. Rumour is that the amendment could get dropped." Vipul added.

"Why should these industrialists oppose protection to poor creatures, robots?" Sevugan could not understand.

"All money power Sevu. They built a big business empire on robotic technology and they will not allow anything that could *throw a spanner* in their business. Unfortunately, this government would not do anything against their wishes as they are heavily dependent on them for the party funds. Politics is a difficult subject to comprehend for robots." Vipul smiled.

"We might go on a strike if the Robot Protection Act is not enacted in this session. Our association has taken the decision."

Vipul was shocked. He did not expect that this issue might lead to a strike by the robots. In fact, nobody ever thought of robots resorting to a strike. That robots would not strike was touted as the big selling point for deploying robots in place of humans. It would be another big hit to the economy in addition to the lockdown if the robots decided to strike. India Inc would come to a halt as robots have replaced many humans in the workplace. There was a news item last month that a robot has become a robotics programmer and is currently working on designing robots. The first robot to create another robot.

"Sevu, don't you know that strikes are banned in India? Even we humans cannot think of resorting to a strike. We would be put in jail." Vipul tried to dissuade Sevugan.

"I am aware that strikes are banned in India. There is an advantage of being a robot. We went through the provisions of the Industrial Enabler Act banning strikes. Strikes are illegal as per provision 2c (ii) of this Act. We noticed that the law states 'group of persons or assembly of persons' and does not mention robots. So, the law does not bind us robots." Sevugan laughed.

Vipul thought to himself, 'Vinitha is correct. I need to be careful with this robot. He is becoming too smart.'

"You anyway have the SPCAR to take care of your interests. Society for Prevention of Cruelty to Animals and Robots is very powerful and they get funds from the government." Vipul explained.

"I am not happy at equating robots with animals. Animals have only five senses and we are created with all six senses. We are not equal to animals. We are forming a separate organization to take care of our interests exclusively." Sevugan said.

"Why do you need any organization to protect you? Are we being cruel to you?" Vipul asked, half out of curiosity and half because he really wanted to be sure.

"Both of you have been nice to me overall. I don't have any issue." Sevugan conceded.

"Sevu, my parents have come. My father is a heart patient and he has to eat before 8 PM. Get back to work. I hope you don't have any grievances cooking for us. We will find it difficult to manage the house if you resort to a strike." Vinitha teased.

Just when this argument was happening, *Abra* sounded the RED alarm and switched on the news item.

A laboratory building came up and the voice announced, "Scientists from the virology lab have decoded the strain and confirmed that the mysterious disease is caused by a virus. This virus is similar in characteristics to the Corona virus identified a hundred years back and hence the new virus is named Covid2121. Scientists are doing further research to find out why this strain is not immune to all the known Covid vaccines. Scientists have advised strict compliance to Corona rules including avoiding social contact, maintaining safe distance, etc. The government announced that those who need to travel must apply for travel permission by attaching necessary documents before 8.00 PM today and the permission, if approved, would be distributed online. Automatic vehicle recognition cameras have been installed at strategic locations and the license of the vehicle captured in the camera without an approved 'lockdown permission' loaded to the vehicle's identification badge would be withdrawn automatically."

This was followed by an update from the Commissioner of Police, Chennai. "Vehicular traffic is banned in all the areas of Chennai and in all the airways leading to Chennai. Citizens are requested not to venture out by car or by flyo unless a valid lockdown license is updated to the identification badge of the vehicle. All monitoring cameras at important junctions have already been programmed to capture the name plates and cancel the license if any vehicle is caught without 'lockdown permission'. All entertainment zones have been closed. **Luz corner beach** and **Adyar beach** have been closed for vehicles as well as pedestrians."

Luz and Adyar are the two popular beaches in Chennai. There used to be a beach called Marina which was the longest beach in Asia once upon a time. There used to be a very popular tourist destination called Mahabalipuram. Both have submerged in the sea.

Vinitha called out, "Vipul, can you check the release notes of Robogenius OS v7.4.1? It must still be available on the net. They normally release a few new features and fix a few known vulnerabilities. I am keen on the list of vulnerabilities fixed in v7.4.1. If you cannot, I will ask my office to get this and send it to me. I need it urgently. I want to explore this but could not do yesterday and today because of the travel and worries about appa's health."

"OK. I will do. But why do you want this info? What will you do with this information?"

"I can decide only after I see the information." Vinitha meant it. "Strange that a patch had to give problem and the next day a new virus is reported. Robogenius had never withdrawn its OS versions or patches earlier." Vinitha explained. "Robogenius is the leader in the industry and would not make such stupid mistakes. I am getting obsessed with the intuition that both are **somehow connected**. I don't have any information to substantiate my intuition." Vinitha added.

FRIDAY, 18TH APRIL 2121

"Good morning, son. The Covid2121 virus is spreading very fast despite a lockdown. Be careful and cooperate with the government by following Covid2121 appropriate behaviour. Stay at home. Don't go out even for purchases. Everything can be delivered to your house, nowadays. Wear Covid2121 appropriate mask all the time except when sleeping," *Abra* announced.

Vipul was curious as well as furious as to how *Abra*'s alarm message got changed. He was very particular about his first wake-up message being the *asheervadam* of Lord Balaji. He did not like waking up to a Covid2121 alert message. Who changed the message? Vinitha's parents would not touch *Abra*. That left Vinitha and Sevugan only. Would it be possible that Sevugan would have fiddled with the configuration? He was always curious about *Abra*. He kept asking Vipul about *Abra* but Vipul told him strictly not to use *Abra*.

When Vipul was thinking about all these, *Abra* played his favourite Lord Balaji *darshan*, blessings message and *abhaya*[1] pose.

Vipul was happy to know that his *asheervadam* was not removed. Someone prefixed his regular 'good morning' routine with another message. He got irritated.

"*Abra*, Good Morning" Vipul wanted to test the routine. *Abra* started "Good morning, son. The Covid2121 virus is spreading…."

"Stop *Abra*," Vipul shouted when the message came to "cooperate with the government".

Neither Vinitha nor Sevugan would configure a message asking for cooperation with the government. Definitely not Vinitha!

Vipul did his morning routine and came to the front room and said "*Abra*. Top 10 News"

Abra again played "Good morning, son. The Covid2121 virus is spreading…." before announcing 'Top 10 News'. He got irritated listening to the message. He immediately logged in to the configuration interface of *Abra* to change the message. He saw a notice that a prefix message was added and he could not delete the added prefix message. Abra announced "High privilege prefix message and requires *super administrator* privilege to change". He realized that this must be the work of the government and

---

[1] abhaya – Hand pose of the Lord giving the assurance that he would protect.

they would have asked the designer to give them the super administrator privilege when giving approval for the design.

He felt ashamed of himself for doubting Vinitha. She was particular about his rights as particular about her space, and so would not change without his knowledge. She may tease him or nag him but would never interfere. With Vinitha, it was always straight batting.

But he could still not accept the government overriding his *asheervad* message. 'It is my personal device and how could government override and manage my personal device.' Vipul thought. *Abra* went to 'Top 10 News of your choice' after playing the prefix alert.

The scorching summer temperature pushed the Covid2121 news to the second spot for the first time that week. The temperature in many cities across India breached the 55°C mark for the first time. The government announced that they were analysing the need to further tighten water rationing.

The government announced that the water quota of 120 litres per citizen per day was likely to get reduced to 100 litres per citizen per day. The government warned that the heat wave would become even more intense during *agni nakshatram*[2] and warned the citizens to take care of all necessary precautions to protect them from extreme heat.

---

[2] Agni Nakshatram – Period of about 25 days in May during which heat will be intense in India.

"How many precautions will we take? precautions galore!... The list appears endless. Our life will be spent in taking precautions all the time. We are anyway not going out because of Covid threat. What is the need for one more warning. The government should do something apart from giving precautions and warnings." Vinitha was not happy

"It is the duty of the government to give us our water need." Varad started the breakfast table discussion for the day.

"But where is the water? All water sources have drained and all rivers shrunk. By the time the government implemented the project to interlink the rivers, the rivers dried." Vinitha explained.

"We are now using only treated sea water and treated wastewater." Vipul added

"I heard rumours that it is possible that an ordinance could come in the next session of the parliament banning the practice of hand wash using water. A private organization identified a water like chemical which could be developed in a chemical reaction at low cost. You need less quantity of this chemical to wash hands and utensils. They are thinking of supplying this to houses through a pipeline. Once this becomes operational, we will have to bathe and wash using a chemical. Henceforth water can be used only for drinking and cooking purposes." Vinitha was a voracious reader and devoured current affairs as we do our daily breakfast. And she gave out her knowledge on current affairs as a 'heads up'.

"The government brings out an ordinance for everything. The speed with which this government enacts new ordinances, even the parliamentarians will lose track of it." Vinitha commented.

"Water is also a chemical. Water is H_2O." Vipul commented.

"Water is a naturally available chemical component." Vinitha added.

"Once this technology becomes available, we will see people settling on the Moon and Mars. The only challenge we face now on the Moon and Mars is the availability of water." Vipul reacted.

"Yes. We already have a travel package taking people to the Moon. It is a one night two days travel package with a night stay on the Moon. We have this tour package available from two space ports in India." Vinitha said.

"I want to go to the Moon once before I die. It is my dream." Varad said.

"It is very much affordable now. There are weekly tour packages offered by many travel companies. But the problem is that there are a few health prerequisites for space travel. People can take the package only after clearing the health tests. I doubt if you will clear the tests in your current condition. Let us wait for some more time." Vinitha offered.

"Have you ever seen a water well? My father used to maintain a well in our house and we had to close the well a couple of years before you were born." Varad went down memory lane.

"Well… our generation, we would not know the meaning of the word 'well'. They would know it well if they had seen it. Well, since they haven't, they don't know about the well." Vipul played his pun.

Varad laughed. "Your generation is missing a lot of fun. If I think back about our younger days, I feel like going back to those days. You people would not have seen a television set, going on vacation with family, etc."

"Uncle, I am tired of hearing this language. My grandfather also used to talk similarly whenever he saw a new technology emerge. The only difference is that he would quote something else which you would have also not seen. But you people end up getting hooked to the same technology more than us. I have seen you getting addicted to Sevugan's services, but you will continue to criticise development of artificial intelligence in robotics. I see you keep trying various games on *Abra*. Don't you?!" Vipul queried.

"Not like that…" Varad could not complete the sentence.

After ensuring that Sevugan was not anywhere near, Vinitha said in a hushed tone, "That reminds me Vipul, I told you to watch out for Sevugan's behaviour. His behaviour today is very strange and I am not comfortable."

"What are you not comfortable with?" Vipul

"Stupid husband. How will I explain it to you? His behaviour, especially with me, does not look normal. His crass looks and funny comments at me."

"What are you worried about? Can you be more specific?"

"He told me today, that too when you were not around, 'Your bathroom song is very nice. You can become a good singer. Your voice is sweeter than your looks'. Unnecessary comment. He is taking undue advantage of your soft nature."

"Vinu. You are getting prejudiced with Sevugan. Remember, he is a robot and not a human. A robot will be more straightforward."

"That is why I am worried. I am more worried because Sevu is a robot."

"You are getting misguided by the entertainment movies showing treacherous robots. They are not practical but crazy imaginations. That happens only in movies. Sevugan is intelligent, no doubt about it. But remember his intelligence is monitored and controlled by us. Robots cannot turn villains. They are controlled by humans, and we know how to control them well. Don't get scared unnecessarily by seeing movies. Since you are at home all the time this week due to lockdown, you are with him most of the time. You are observing him closely now, but he is always like that."

"Coming to think about it, Sevugan seems to be correct. I never realised it" Vipul smiled but Vinitha became even more furious.

"Don't be sure of that, Vipul. Always be cautious. Remember, as a cyber security person, I get to see a lot of the wrong side of technology. When the computers were first put to commercial use in late twentieth century, nobody imagined that a computer application can turn treacherous. But today it is possible. Any application can be made to misbehave and give dangerous results. That is why we, the breed of cyber security engineers, are in great demand now."

"I agree. But if you are afraid that Sevugan is making sexual advances, you can be 100% sure that it is unwarranted and not possible. Sexual orientation is completely disabled and deactivated in Next Generation Robots."

"I am not sure about that. I know that it can be changed. Attackers are ever vigilant and are waiting for the first opportunity to strike."

"Hackers can manipulate applications but how would they manipulate when the robots cannot feel about sex. It is blocked in the design of the Next Generation Robots."

"*Zero Trust*[3] is the first lesson for us in cyber security. We deploy Zero Trust Architecture. I cannot trust that Next Generation Robots are designed for absolute security. We must always be on our guard."

---

[3] Zero Trust principle - Zero Trust is a security framework requiring all users, whether in or outside the organization's network, to be authenticated, authorized and continuously validated for security configuration and posture before being granted or keeping access to applications and data.

"If Zero Trust is the core principle of cyber security, trust is the core principle of leadership. Zero Trust can be OK for cyber security but we cannot run an organization by Zero Trust."

"You are getting confused, Vipul. Zero Trust principle does not mean never to trust. Zero Trust principle is not to permit unless confirmed beyond doubt as trusted. I need to take a lesson for you on Zero Trust. The key here is not to depend on **implicit trusts**. I have a vague feeling that you are going by implicit trust in the case of Sevugan."

"OK. Still fine. Trust me that I am very confident of his trustworthiness." Vipul tried to bring the discussion to an end.

"Don't assume. Don't assume, as you always do, that I started this discussion based on presumptions." After looking here and there and ensuring that Sevugan could not hear them, Vinitha said in low voice, "Do you know that Sevugan is sitting here with a known vulnerability, and he can be made to behave in anyway if a smart attacker comes to know of that vulnerability?"

"What is this story?" Vipul asked.

"This is not a story. This is cyber security intelligence. You will understand this only if you know how to appreciate cyber security professionals."

"OK. I agree. You guys are 'God-sent' breed. Tell me more about this vulnerability."

"It is known as Remote Code Execution vulnerability."

"What is Remote Code Execution? Explain it to me."

"Before explaining that, I initially thought that his behaviour change is because of the buggy patch released by Robogenius. Now I am worried if any attacker is exploiting his vulnerability. Are you sure? Sevugan is still running with the old version of the OS?" Vinitha asked.

"100% sure. Sevugan can be configured for auto patch update or manual patch update. I consciously configured him for manual patch update so that I can update after making sure of the stability of the patch. I update to one older version of the patch when a new patch gets released. The buggy patch 7.4.1 was released last Tuesday, I don't know why they released a new patch a day before Tamil New Year. I updated Sevugan to 7.4.0 from 7.3.9 on Tuesday after seeing the alert message about the new patch release. I am 100% sure." Vipul replied.

"I researched yesterday on 7.4.1 release notes of Robogenius Robatma OS home edition. This patch was released primarily to fix *Remote Code Execution* vulnerability. It is quite strange that a vulnerability fix can turn out to be buggy. We have never heard of such a possibility, especially with a global leader like Robogenius. I asked Robogenius to give me more information about the bug, but not received any reply yet."

"They will not give. They have never given. I love their products but not their transparency. This is not strange. Robogenius is well known to release software with bugs."

"But not in a patch that is released to fix a vulnerability. This means Sevugan is still vulnerable for Remote Code Execution. You are keeping him vulnerable because of your great strategy of running with one patch level less." Vinitha smiled.

"Don't blame me for everything. Now that they have withdrawn the new version, I don't have an option to upgrade to a new version."

"What is Remote Code Execution? If he is vulnerable to Remote Code Execution, will he shoot us with a gun like what we saw in the Rajinikanth starrer movie *Robo*?" Varad was worried that he couldn't manage to win over Sevugan's agility at his advanced age. "I will not go anywhere near Sevugan until Robogenius releases the new patch which will work without any bug and also fix that stupid vulnerability."

"Anything is possible. Depends on how the attacker manages to exploit the vulnerability. Remote Code Execution vulnerability means a weakness in code design using which an attacker can remotely execute commands on Sevugan. His behaviour can change depending on the attacker's malicious code running in the robot." Vinitha took a mini lesson on cyber security.

"I never thought about this. Why cannot Robogenius fix the bug quickly rather than withdrawing the patch?" Vipul asked with a serious concern.

"Apparently, Robogenius is still not able to find out the reason for the bug and that is why they are not able to fix the bug." Vinitha quickly added.

"What do we do then?"

"I would suggest cutting off all internet access for Sevugan until Robogenius fixes the Remote Code Execution vulnerability."

"Not possible. Sevugan requires internet access to get updates, synch calendars & instructions. Without internet access, Sevugan will become an idiotic robot."

"If that is the case, you can selectively allow only what is required and block others. That is possible using the *firewall*[4] in the NGN robot."

"I don't know how to configure this in Sevugan. I will check. But he will feel bad if we cut off his internet access suddenly and he might not cooperate with us."

"Disconnect Internet access until a fix for the vulnerability is released. Must be quick. It is always a trade-off between security and functionality."

"I will find out." Vipul's answer was meek.

"Don't get too carried away by his utility and intelligence, it is artificial intelligence."

"By the way, have you hardened Sevugan?" Vinitha suddenly remembered.

"Hardening Sevugan is not required. Sevugan is very hard already. Though his skin looks like human skin, it is very hard.

---

[4] firewall – Firewall is a component which monitors traffic in and out and blocks or allows based on predefined rules.

Try throwing a stone at Sevugan. The stone will break but nothing will happen to Sevugan." Vipul was excited.

"Stop the nonsense, Vipul. I am talking about ensuring enough security controls." Vinitha signalled him to stop.

"How will configuring security controls be known as hardening?"

"Probably because hardening makes a device stronger to resist attacks." Vinitha raised her hand as if she was not very sure of her explanation.

"I really thought hardening means making his body tougher. I am not joking. What is hardening? Explain."

"Hardening is the process of reducing attack surface." Vinitha started another lesson on cyber security, but Vipul stopped her.

"This is the problem with you cyber security engineers. You immediately jump to jargons and make it very difficult for ordinary people like me to understand. You must learn how to explain it in an understandable language. Attack surface, I only know the surface area. If you are talking about outside surface area, Sevugan has larger surface area compared to an average robot. Do you remember, we selected big build when giving our preference?"

"Ayyo!" Vinitha made a gesture to hit him and close his mouth.

"Reducing attack surface means reducing the possibilities of security attacks by removing weaknesses." Vinitha explained.

"This is better. Now, I understand. Talk like this. We are ignorant on cyber security. You must talk in our language."

"OK Professor. I will do exactly as per your command." Vinitha laughed. "Come to the point. Have you hardened Sevugan?"

"I told you I don't even know the meaning of hardening. How can I harden without knowing what is hardening?"

"It is quite popular now. You have enough checklists and procedures for 'hardening a robot'. I will download and give you a checklist. Please ensure to harden at once." Vinitha warned.

"OK. Give me the details and I will attend to this immediately. I don't want Sevugan to run around inside the house with a pistol in his hand."

"Not a laughing matter Vipul. Be serious. People take security seriously in house robots as well. We now get requests for vulnerability assessments for house robots as well. We developed an automatic tool to check and alert vulnerabilities in a house robot."

"You never told me all these. I thought nothing can happen to a house robot."

"There is a lot you don't know boss." Vinitha closed the conversation.

The discussion then shifted to the progress of child license. Vinitha updated her parents about further process.

Vipul conveniently forgot about internet access for Sevugan as Vinitha switched to different discussion.

The first consultation post the license approval happened the previous day. The first consultation was bundled with the cost of the license registration. Consultation was also virtual, not because of the lockdown. Most of the consultation happens virtual unless an intrusive procedure is required. Most of the diagnostics also happen virtual. Doctors can virtually inspect various parts of the body using a highly sensitive touchpad, hear accurate pulse & heartbeat, even measure blood pressure & ECG remotely. Almost everything except an intrusive procedure such as surgery.

A special diagnostic device similar to a watch is a mandatory requirement for all virtual diagnostics. This device is used by remote health care specialists for checking all the vitals including pulse, blood pressure, etc. This device comes with a pen sized PTZ[5] camera which can be controlled remotely for all physical examinations. This device has a special pad in the strap which can be used by doctors to sense the skin, reflex, etc. X-ray scanning is also possible with this device and the X-ray patterns can be immediately seen on the screen. Vinitha purchased a diagnostic watch for her father so that she could monitor their vitals remotely.

Vipul and Vinitha had to undergo the first consultation. They had been prescribed medicines for gene therapy based on their

---

[5] PTZ – Pan, Tilt & Zoom

final agreed gene matching. The government made it mandatory for the couple to willingly participate in gene therapy by enacting a law in the parliament. Progress of gene therapy shall be monitored and signs if any found of not participating in the gene therapy could lead to cancelation of childbirth license and even punishment in a court of law.

Birth control restrictions can be stopped only after confirmation of first consultation so that gene therapy would have started before conception.

The doctor advised Vipul and Vinitha that they should be ready for conception in a month and can stop all the control measures after the second consultation in which the progress of gene therapy would be reviewed. Medicine as per the prescription got delivered at home the previous day due to lockdown restrictions. Gene therapy prescriptions include medicines which leave tell-tale signs in the system so that the medical controllers can test and confirm that the prescribed gene therapy is followed and not circumvented.

-X-X-X

Vinitha broached the topic at the dinner table "I feel like withdrawing from the license. I don't feel comfortable with the government monitoring and controlling my pregnancy. It is too much of an intrusion into my privacy."

"Are you crazy? We will be pushed to the last in the queue and a two-year waiting period will be added if we withdraw now. These controls are applicable to everyone. Nobody can escape these.

And there is nothing new in this. These procedures are in vogue for the last ten years and are getting improved every year." Vipul consoled her.

"I will be happy if I am left alone. We are not genetically corrected children Vipul. We are doing well and there is nothing wrong with us. Why do we need gene correction? Why is the government so particular about gene correction?

"Because the Indian government wants to make India a superpower in all aspects by 2150. This is a project called Mission 2150 and the insistence on gene therapy is an essential part of this project. The government thinks that gene therapy is a means to create super-humans, intelligent, athletic, successful Indians. All the developed nations follow this, and India is a developed nation. You must have heard that India overtook USA in GDP[6] terms and has become the top economy in the world. Gene therapy has become a *rat race* now." Vipul explained.

"India is already ahead of USA. Why do they enforce birth control and birth license? It is unfair" Varad questioned.

"Unacceptable." Vinitha corrected.

"Though India has become the leading economy in GDP terms, we are still far behind other developed countries in terms of *'per*

---

[6] GDP – Gross Domestic Product, monetary measure of the market value of all the final goods and services produced and sold

capita income[7] due to our large population. Our PM's vision is to make India the leader in 'per capita income' as well"

"By snatching away our 'right to beget our progenies'?" Vinitha would not accept that easily.

"India is already a superpower; our government believes that India's economic growth was achieved only because of India's supremacy in Information Technology. Our Prime Minister does not want India to be overly reliant on Information Technology. He has the vision and the blueprint to make India a superpower in every field." Vipul added unmindful of Vinitha's opinion.

"How does it matter if India achieves superpower status only because of supremacy in Information Technology? Let it be." Varad said.

"It will not be a sustainable development as per the vision of our Prime Minister. He wants integrated and sustainable development, i.e. development in every field." Vipul explained.

"That cannot be vision. You cannot aspire to become a superpower by fixing genes. That is like playing with fire." Vinitha argued.

"I agree with you. But we don't have any choice now. We don't get an option to opt out." Vipul is ever a law-abiding citizen.

---

[7] per capita income - amount of money earned per individual in a nation

Varad intervened in their conversation with a message, "*Mapillai*[8], do you know that the government made an announcement today that they are temporarily withdrawing birth license approvals until further advice? They don't want to take any chance until the virus issue settles. This announcement came just five minutes back."

"Oh God! Will this apply to our approval as well? Must be." Vipul fiddled with his mobile phone to see the messages from the government. The government has a separate high priority interface with instant messaging in all the phone services to send announcements. There were a couple of high priority alerts and one of the alerts as expected said:

"Your birth license is suspended due to unforeseen virus issues. Do not stop your birth control prescription. You will get information as soon as the HOLD is removed. Thanks for your understanding and support."

The same message was there in Vinitha's Inbox as well as a High Priority Alert in flashing red.

"Oh God, what to do now?" Vinitha was exhausted.

"Nothing to do, wait and pray that Covid2121 will go away now."

"I am not sure if the government is doing enough to bring down Covid2121. The existing vaccines are not effective. We might

---

[8] Mapillai – Tamil word indicating the relationship 'Son-in-law'

have to wait until a new vaccine is found and tested. That process will take months." Vinitha explained.

"We then have to wait for months and hope that the time will fly fast." Vipul never showed emotions, but Vinitha could not hide her disappointment. There was pin drop silence for a couple of minutes. Vipul first broke the silence with an enthusiastic message.

"I forgot to update you. I had booked for Balaji *arjitha seva* tomorrow as a *prarthana* to our child license and Varadappa becoming alright. We are lucky to get *arjitha seva* on a Saturday. It is good that we got four tickets for tomorrow, your father and mother can also join. We must be prepared and be ready in front of *Abra* before 5 AM. *arjitha seva* starts exactly at 5 AM. They will not allow entry after 4.50 AM."

"You did not tell me, and it sounds to be the wrong time now. I thought I will take it very easy tomorrow, it being a Saturday. Now I must get up early." Vinitha was not very happy. She was more disturbed by the news about the cancellation of the license.

"Don't talk like that Vinu. There must be some reason for this postponement which Lord Balaji would only know. Join the *seva* tomorrow and pray sincerely and Covid2121 will go away quickly." Vijaya consoled her by placing her hands on her shoulder.

"Yes. We have to take a bath and assemble in front of *Abra* by 4.45 AM in the hall." Vipul clarified.

"It is virtual anyway. They cannot sense if I had taken bath or not. I am not going to take a bath so early. You do whatever you want. I have no issues." Vinitha protested.

Vipul left it at that as he knew that it would be difficult to convince Vinitha.

Abra started a Red Alert message.

"Covid2121 has taken away lives of one million people globally, so far. 52 countries have declared complete lockdown and emergency, but the spread is not slowing down. With this rate of increase, every citizen of India would be affected by Covid2121 in another forty days. Heads of G7 countries had an important virtual meeting this morning and agreed for global cooperation to bring this pandemic under control. Heads of G7 have reposed faith in India's capabilities in controlling the virus as the biotech capital of the world."

A newsflash came up on the screen with the tag High Priority Alert. The Chief Minister of Tamil Nadu came on the screen and started reading his message with a *vanakkam*. He first explained the challenges posed by the deadly virus Covid2121 and how the government of Tamil Nadu was taking proactive steps to control the virus. He claimed that Tamil Nadu is the leader among all the states in India in controlling Covid2121. He went on to substantiate his claim by projecting a graph that showed bars of varying heights and the bar against the label Tamil Nadu was the longest. At the same time a High Priority Alert in a house on the outskirts of Bengaluru showed the Chief Minister of Karnataka claiming after a *namaskara*, that Karnataka is leading among all the states in Covid2121 control and the graph projected by him had similar bars but the bar against the label Karnataka was the longest!

SATURDAY, 19ᵀᴴ APRIL 2121

Everyone in the family assembled before *Abra* by 4.55 AM and logged into the virtual *seva* portal by giving their face as well as biometric authentication. The *seva* portal would keep validating all the people within the coverage of the camera to check if anyone without a valid ticket had joined the *seva*. If any additional human was found, the screen would go blank until the person left the area.

The *seva* started with *thirumanjanam*[1] for Lord Balaji.

"This is very good but still nothing like visiting the temple. We used to go to Tirumala every year. The spiritual vibration of going to Tirumala is a unique experience." Varad reminisced.

---

[1] thirumanjanam – Holy bath given to the Lord.

"They have now changed all the *sevas* to *shadverse* mode. Only one *seva*, VIP *seva*, is available at the temple and they made *shadverse* experience much better than a visit to the temple. You will get an opportunity to touch the feet of Lord Balaji which you would have never experienced in your visits to the temple. We have a very good resolution touchpad and you can look forward to this divine experience today. Wait and experience the miracle." Vipul kindled their curiosity.

"*Mapillai,* is there an option to offer my *manjathuni mudichu* in the virtual *seva*?" Vijaya asked.

Vipul was not sure if it was a joke or an innocent question but replied seriously, "Technology has still not advanced to send material through the wire. That might become a reality in the next decade."

"My colleague from our Delhi office used to invariably ask during our virtual meetings if I can make it possible to send my south Indian filter coffee through the Internet. He is a big fan of filter coffee and he cracks the same joke whenever he senses the aroma of my coffee during meetings. It will be interesting to see this becoming a reality. He will at least stop cracking the same joke in all the meetings." Vinitha laughed.

"It is not a laughing matter. I remember reading a technology update that IIT-Madras is doing a research project on using the Internet for automatic delivery of material." Vipul added.

"How would this be feasible? I cannot comprehend. Must be a crude joke." Vinitha responded.

"They have not given more details. It could probably be like sending some codes and triggering micro drones to deliver and return. Any technology innovation when first proposed sounds like a joke only."

"Varadappa, can you imagine thirty years back that *shadverse* would be possible? You would have probably thought it to be a joke." Vipul said.

"Hundred percent true. Such a technology could be possible, Vinu. Why do you think it should be a joke? Anyway, where better than IIT-Madras to try to send filter coffee through Internet?" Varad cracked a joke and everyone had a hearty laugh.

The *seva* got over in 45 minutes with the ritual of each devotee virtually touching Lord Balaji's feet and seeking his blessings at the end of the *seva*. This was followed by an opportunity to touch the *kalpoorarthi*[2] and take the *sadari*[3] on their head. All four of them symbolically placed their hand above the plate with *kalpoora deepam* and lowered their heads to take the *sadari*.

Vijaya by mistake touched the *kalpoora deepam* and got light burns on her palm.

Vipul said, "amma is not used to *kalpoorarthi* in *shadverse* mode. She would have assumed it to be a simulation of *kalpoorarthi*. Everything is real in *shadverse* mode."

---

[2] kalpoorarthi – Offering to the Lord given with burning camphor.
[3] sadari – A silver object symbolic of the Lord's feet.

"*Mapillai,* as you said, putting my head on Lord Balaji's feet was a divine experience. I involuntarily touched my head to see if the oil from the Lord's feet was there on my head." Varad was ecstatic.

"All fine. Where is our *prasadam*[4]? Balaji *darshan* can never get over without eating the delicious *laddus*. *Prasadam* is a very important part of a Perumal *koil* visit." Vijaya said with a smile.

"Not to worry amma. Our *prasadam* will get delivered to our house in just two hours direct from Tirumala temple by a temple *archaka*[5]. See the fun in two hours." Vipul added a curiosity quotient.

"Do they have enough *archakas* to send to all the *sevarthis*, they might be needing many of them?" Vijaya queried.

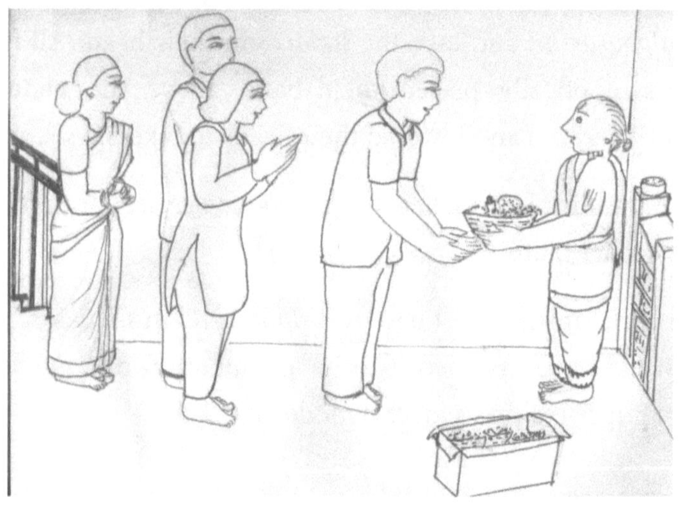

---

[4] prasadam – Food offered to the Lord, laddu is a very popular prasadam at Tirumala.
[5] archaka – Temple priest in a Vaishnavaite temple.

"No. They are short of *archakas*. They use specially designed next generation robots dressed as *archakas*. You would not have guessed it if I had not told you." Vipul beamed.

As he said, an *archaka* with a typical Tirumala *namam*[6] on his forehead, dressed in a white *veshti*[7] in *panjakatcham*[8] style, with his long tuft tied behind and dangling from his head, came into the house with four bamboo baskets in his hands. He handed over the *prasadam* after chanting the *asservada mantram* to each one of them. The *prasadam* basket included a *laddu*, a *vadai*, a *thulasi mala*, flowers and *thirumanjana jalam*[9] in a small bottle.

Just when the *archaka* was leaving the hall, he saw Sevugan entering with a tray of glasses filled with water.

"Is he not included in the *seva?*" the *archaka* asked.

"No. He is a robot. Robots do not belong to any religion, and we cannot subject them to religious practices as per the Robot Control Act." Vipul clarified. He was worried that he would be blamed for not including Sevugan in the *seva*.

"I am a robot and I perform all religious duties to Lord Balaji."

"Tirumala temple has taken special exemption for their robots. We individuals, will not get such exemption." Vipul clarified. Vipul was not comfortable with the robot priest asking

---

[6] namam – Symbol known as thiruman used by Vaishnavaites, followers of Lord Vishnu, on their forehead. Thiruman (sacred sand) is the religious name and namam is the colloquial name.
[7] veshti - A traditional white cloth wrapped around the lower part of the body.
[8] panjakatcham – Traditional way of dressing in a veshti during religious ceremonies.
[9] thirumanjana jalam – Sacred water used to bathe the Lord.

unnecessary questions in front of Sevugan. He was worried that it would add to Sevugan's rebellious nature.

"Does not matter. We have the privilege to give free *asservadam* to one family member. I will use that privilege to wish this robot brother," the *archaka* said.

The *archaka* called Sevugan and garlanded him and recited the *asservada mantram* for Sevugan also. "Anyway, we don't consume or enjoy *laddus*." The *archaka* kept his hand on Sevugan's head and left.

"Robot to robot affection. *Birds of a feather flock together!*" Vipul exclaimed.

"I felt as if a real temple *archaka* gave us the *asservadam*. Hard to believe that it is a robot!" Varad exclaimed.

"Yes, uncle. The *devasthanam* has mapped the complete behaviour of the *archakas* and has designed the robots. TTD and Robogenius formed a special initiative for this project."

"By the way, how did he come so fast within two hours?" Vijaya asked.

"Temple robots are designed to fly. They can fly on their own. They don't require a separate flyo."

"How did he find our house; I would not be able to find our house easily though I have come here several times?" Vijaya asked.

"Because you are not a next generation robot. They take the download of the UDIC of all the registered *sevarthis* and download the route map of their registered houses *from Babool maps*".

"It is difficult to find people nowadays wearing *thiruman*[1]. Nobody wears it. And that *panjakatcham* was very perfect. I forgot how to wear *panjakatcham* as *veshtis* are not available for purchase now." Varad said.

"His *panjakatcham veshti* during our marriage kept slipping frequently leaving his underwear visible. Finally, my father tied his own belt around his waist and the *veshti* remained firm only after that." Vijaya teased Varad.

"What to do? I dread two things when I think about that unfortunate event. One was my travails with *panjakatcham* and the other was the subordination and teasing by this woman lifelong." Varad teased back.

Vipul smiled observing their intimacy. Very comfortable teasing each other. No ego at all between them. It was difficult to find couples like them.

"I had no such problem, the practice of wearing *panjakatcham* was not there during my marriage. I was saved. But the other part is true in my case as well." Vipul interfered to change the topic.

"Even human *archakas* no longer wear their *veshti* in *panjakatcham* style. They use ready-stitched *panjakatcham* type of *veshti*. This robot was wearing a nice original *panjakatcham* style. But still a robot is a robot. A robot cannot get the sanctity to perform the Lord's duties." Varad still could not comprehend the fact that he received *asservadam* from a robot.

"Do you know uncle, that many of the *pujas* and *sevas* are now handled by robots? They have been trained for most of the *sevas*. It is possible that the *thirumanjanam* we watched today may have been performed by robots. We will not know. It is difficult to verify in a virtual *seva*." Vipul laughed.

"What are you saying *mapillai*? How can a robot perform *thirumanjanam*? Ridiculous. What happened to our *acharams* and *anushtanams*[10]? How could a robot touch the sacred body of Lord Balaji? How could a robot remain pure before touching Lord Balaji? Can a robot take a head bath? *Archakas* have to take head bath and wear a *madi*[11] *veshti* before they can touch the Lord." Varad was agitated.

"What is a *madi veshti* uncle? Is it an ironed *veshti*? They can keep the *veshtis* ironed. That would not be a problem." Vipul was confused as to what language his father-in-law used in between.

Varad was flabbergasted. "*Abacharam*, a *Srivaishnavaite* who does not know the meaning of *madi veshti*."

"I don't even know what *Srivaishnavaite* means. You keep repeating the same word. Let me first try to pronounce it. I don't know if I will get it correctly." Vipul said.

---

[10] acharams and anushtanams – Observance of religious rites and daily religious practices.
[11] madi - Classical and religious language used to refer to pure & clean dresses.

Varad looked at him as if he did not want to continue that conversation thread. "It is my fault. I did not brief you enough about our *sampradayam*[12]."

"No need uncle. I am fine and happy with whatever I can be. I am spiritual and I revere Lord Balaji and I am very fond of our culture and heritage. That is more than sufficient for and I don't feel bad that I don't understand the so called *sampradayam*" Vipul retorted.

Varad kept quiet and felt bad for having taken up the topic.

Vipul understood the impact of his retort and changed the subject "Tirumala robots are waterproof, and they have been programmed to take a head bath before entering the *sanctum sanctorum*. I was told that they built a separate bathing ghat abutting the *pushkarni*[13] where the robots get showered with a spray daily before entering the temple. Human *archakas* might miss taking a head bath on some days but the robots will never miss the head bath even for a day, not even in the cold December month. They are cleaner and better disciplined than humans. I heard that they built a sensor at the entrance of the temple and the sensor will sound if any robot entering the temple has not taken a bath in the last 24 hours." Vipul gave a lecture.

Sevugan was silently listening to this exchange. He intruded at this point. "There is no need for us robots to take a bath. You humans take a bath to cleanse your body as it gets impure fast.

---

[12] sampradayam – Religious tradition.
[13] pushkarani – Tank with divine water.

We don't take food. We don't sweat. Out of the five *karmendriyas*, only three *karmendriyas*: speech, grasping and walking ie mouth, hands and feet are applicable to us robots. We don't need the other two *karmendriyas* namely excretion and procreation as we don't generate any waste and we are not designed for reproduction. So, the only way we get impure is dust accumulating on the outer skin which can be cleansed by dusting. We don't need to take a bath. Still, they made our brethren to take a bath just to satisfy you, humans. Strange, you are still not satisfied." Sevugan gave a long lecture and most of the humans there could not understand the meaning of many terms mentioned by Sevugan.

"What is this strange word you mentioned, *karme* something?" Vipul asked.

"*Karmendriya*, means, organs or means of action in a human in the Sanskrit language." Sevugan explained.

Varad was not satisfied with the explanation given by Sevugan. "*Kali muthi pochi*[14]. I would think twice before going to Tirumala hereafter."

"What is your problem uncle? You are happy eating the food cooked by me but not OK to receive *prasadam* from a robot. Illogical." Sevugan protested.

"That is..." Varad could not think of any answer.

---

[14] kali muthi pochu – Kaliyuga is the last (fourth) yugam. 'Kali muthi pochu' is a Tamil saying to denote that it is becoming very bad in Kaliyuga compared to the previous yugas.

"You humans are finicky about unnecessary things; you end up missing the rationale. Purity as per our religious scripts refers to purity of mind and thoughts, not necessarily the body. Purity is avoiding bad behaviours - *kama, krodha, lobha, madha, moha* and *matsarya*. You don't bother about these but talk about trivial things like taking a bath, wearing *madi veshti*, etc. We robots are devoid of these bad behaviours by design." Sevugan opened a new argument and every human there was stunned and had no counter.

"What are these? I know the meaning of a few but not all. *Kamam* and *krodham* are very common but not the others." Varad was ashamed of himself that he had to learn from a robot.

"They are known as *shadripu* in our *sastras. Shadripu* means six enemies of the mind. They are excessive desire, anger, greed, arrogance, delusion and jealousy. Anyone who eliminates these enemies is pure. That way, robots are better placed to perform religious duties compared to humans. We don't know the feeling of any of these six enemies."

Every human there instantly became jealous of Sevugan. Vipul offered a meek response, "Where did you learn all these?"

"I got interested in the *Bhagavad Gita*[15]. I am going through the *Bhagavad Gita* verses and various interpretations of the *Bhagavad Gita*."

---

[15] Bhagavad Gita – Song of God, a treatise on dharma (management as well) given by Lord Krishna to Arjuna on the battlefield.

"In how many things will you be getting interested? A couple of days back you were interested in Tamil literature, now in the *Bhagavad Gita*. At this rate, you will become a master of all subjects soon." Vipul looked at Vinitha's face when saying that.

"Sevu, you said *kama*, excessive desire is an enemy. But you seem to be developing an excessive desire for learning. Robots will also get used to the six enemies." Vinitha laughed.

"No madam. Excessive desire for learning will never become an enemy. The *Bhagavad Gita* proclaims learning to be a positive trait in another *sloka*. One should develop a passionate desire for learning, continuous learning. You should never reduce your desire for learning. We are designed with a desire for learning, **machine learning**[16]." Sevugan gave a lecture.

"I did read the *Bhagavad Gita* after retirement, but I don't remember any mention of the six enemies. I remember the detailed explanation in *Gita* about the difference between our body and soul and that the soul never dies, etc. Do robots have a soul, *mapillai?*"

"We don't have any soul. Our soul is our battery. Unlike humans, our soul dies the moment the battery is removed. That way, we don't have to be worried about the cycle of birth and death. Our body anyway goes to an authorized e-waste recycler once we die

---

[16] Machine learning - Computer systems that are able to learn and adapt based on experience without having to write explicit instructions as codes.

unlike *swargam* and *naragam*[17] in the case of humans. You can write a new *Bhagavad Gita* for robots." Sevugan smiled.

"The fear, rather conscience, about *punyam* and *papam*[18], *swargam* and *naragam*, etc., are the check and balance created by God. My fear now is that you don't have any such fear, rather, conscience." Varad made a casual reference. Sevugan gave an expression indicating that he did not exactly like that statement.

Vipul tried to divert the unpleasant direction the conversation was taking. "No options. They don't get enough humans to recruit as *archakas*. Many temples have shut because they could not recruit *archakas*. They increased the salaries and benefits for temple priests but are still not getting enough people. For the past few generations, *archakas* have given their children education and their progenies have become IT professionals. Tirumala has only 20% of its sanctioned strength as human *archakas*. Robots have become a boon now for Tirumala. Otherwise, they would have stopped many *sevas*."

"If they are not getting enough male priests, why cannot they appoint female priests? They will not do that. I am going to file a case in the Supreme Court on this along with my friends." Vinitha opened her pet discussion topic.

---

[17] swargam & naragam – As per Hindu belief, souls who perform good deeds during their life go to a happy place called swargam after their death and souls who accumulate bad deeds suffer torture at naragam.

[18] punyam and papam – Accounting system as per Hindu scripts where good deeds translate to punyam and bad deeds translate to papam.

"You will not win *kanna*. Our scriptures do not permit women to offer *sevas*." Varad said.

"Why not? Let me understand."

"Difficult to explain." Varad was uncomfortable.

"It is OK. I will tell you. Women have the problem of the menstruation cycle." Vipul did not hesitate.

"We have already made a beginning to realize that robots can be considered pure and chaste to perform *pujas*. Why women cannot be considered pure during the menstruation cycle? It is after all a natural phenomenon. Women are anyway comparatively better than men in *shadripu* as mentioned by Sevugan."

"I don't want to comment. But don't assume that it is easy to get women *archakas*. The IT profession employs more women than men. We find it difficult to get women for other jobs. You can probably deploy women robots. That is possible." Vipul said.

"It is a beginning made at Tirumala. All temples will soon turn to robots, at least all the rich temples. All rich temples will go to *shadverse seva* with robots to perform *pujas* in due course. Srirangam Ranganathar temple is testing temple robots now." Vipul clarified.

"Oh Ranganatha. See the status of the *sampradayam* preserved by *Srimad Ramanujar*[19]. *Srimad Ramanujar would turn in his grave.*" Varad was not satisfied.

"*Sankarar*[20] and *Ramanujar* would also have adopted the same tactic if they were alive now. They would have employed robots for their *ashram* work. All humans have become IT professionals, there are no labourers, people not available to do agriculture. Agriculture is dying. There are not enough people for other professions. We will then end up importing all our food requirements." Vinitha said.

"The Central Government is planning to increase the income tax rate of IT professionals by another 10% in the upcoming budget." Vipul reminded her. "We must rework our budgets and savings. Both of us are IT professionals and this increase will hit us hard."

Since all of them got up early for the *seva*, they assembled at the breakfast table earlier than the usual time. *Abra* started the morning news update by the time they had assembled at the breakfast table.

Just when Sevugan was bringing the breakfast dishes to the table, *Abra* beeped the red signal and the announcement started with the hologram of the Scientific Advisor to the Minister of Health. A laboratory could be seen in the background with the smell of laboratory chemicals entering their nostrils.

---

[19],[20] Sankarar & Ramanujar – Two famous proponents from South India who propagated the Bhakti movement in the 8th century and 11th century respectively.

"Scientists have identified the new virus to be a highly contagious disease spreading from human to human. WWO has upgraded the status of Covid2121 to **pandemic** as it is wildly spreading across the globe. India and USA, the top two economies of the world are the worst affected. India strongly refutes the claim made by the Director General of WWO that the first case of Covid2121 was reported from Bengaluru, India. The Government of India claims that the number of infections is high in India because it is reporting the numbers transparently unlike many other countries. As per the reports reaching us, the data from some of the other countries are inadequate and possibly manipulated," the Scientific Advisor announced.

"India's 'R value[21]' has increased to 1.6 as per the available statistics. There are four lakh new infections reported for the day today in India." Graphs with the image of the virus strain in the watermark in the screen appeared as grotesque as it was scary.

"Citizens of India need not panic. Don't worry about the numbers getting reported. Our testing and reporting system is very strong and transparent and that is the reason for India going to the top of the table in terms of the total number of infections. The Government of India is taking every possible step to contain the virus and treat the people who are reporting as infected. All citizens are requested to cooperate with the government in the best interest of the progress of India."

---

[21] R Value - is the number of people that one infected person will pass on a virus to, on average

"It is also identified that the vaccines known to be effective against Covid19 are not protecting against Covid2121 as the current strain is different. The Government of India is making every effort to prepare, test and release an effective vaccine for Covid2121 soon. India is the scientific capital of the world, and we will be the first to bring a vaccine for Covid2121," claimed the Health Minister to the Government of India.

The Health Minister then talked about the need for enforcing strict lockdown and requested all citizens to remain at home and wear special Covid2121 masks even at home. He took out one Covid2121 special mask from his shirt pocket and explained the special features of the Covid2121 mask and that this was different from the one regularly used to protect from pollution. He then stood up and started walking towards Vipul. Vipul was startled. He also stood up not knowing how to respond. The health minister stood right in front of Vipul, took out the same mask from his shirt pocket and put it on Vipul's face. He demonstrated the right procedure for wearing the Covid2121 masks. He even lowered the mask below the nose of Vipul and explained that wearing the mask so was of no use. After completing the demo, the health minister walked back to the screen. Vipul involuntarily touched his nose to check if there was really a mask on his face, but there was none. He felt foolish. Being a robotics engineer, he knew the power of 3D. But the quality of the demo was so good that it left even persons like him deeply impressed. He was surprised. Gone were the days when corporates were the epitome of quality. In today's world, the best technology was accessible first to the government.

SUNDAY, 20ᵀᴴ APRIL 2121

Vipul and his in-laws assembled before Abra late evening. It was time for the Wimbledon finals match. Vinitha was not in a mood to watch the tennis match and hence locked herself in her office room.

"How would they conduct a tennis match in the midst of Covid2121 lockdown?" Varad asked.

"This match is going to be played on a virtual playground. Both the finalists will be playing in their own virtual playgrounds at their homes. I will explain to you what a virtual playground is. This is already popular in tennis and there are attempts to bring virtual playground option in other ball games like badminton and table tennis." Vipul explained about a virtual playground.

Covid2121 struck the world when the Wimbledon tournament was in progress. The organizers had to cancel all the physical matches, send the players quickly back to their countries and convert the rest of the matches to virtual mode.

The virtual playground technique was earlier used by budding players to get sufficient match practice with the seniors. Virtual matches were very popular as a training tool as the trainees could get the opportunity to play against experienced seniors with the seniors playing from their home. Otherwise, it would not be possible to book senior players to come to the training centers for training the juniors. Almost all the popular training academies have established virtual playgrounds on their campuses. Top seeded players had established their own virtual playgrounds at their homes or local clubs. Wimbledon has more than one virtual playground to schedule virtual matches between seeded players at times.

In a virtual match, both the players can play from their nearest virtual playground and the umpires and line umpires can take part from their home settings. The players must make arrangements for their own ball boys in their virtual playground.

Virtual playground is a full tennis court at both locations with dimensions and guidelines as prescribed by the Global Lawn Tennis Association. The playgrounds need to be inspected and approved by the respective Tennis Association. Powerful cameras, microphones, speakers and a high-power supercomputer are essential prerequisites for building a virtual playground. All the rackets used for the play should have powerful sensors permanently attached to the rackets to measure vital parameters like power of the shot, angle, swing force, etc.

When one player plays a shot, the computer monitors the angle, swing, direction and power of the shot, the angle at which the ball is hit using the sensors in the racket and quickly transmits all these computations and the rest of the details to the computer at the other end using high bandwidth links. The computer at the other end picks up the information and translates the information about necessary parameters for the shot that is in terms of power, angle of the hit, swing of the racket, etc., into an image visible to the other player. A ball is quickly released at the receiver's end from the ball holder from a point where it would have entered the receiver's side of the court from the screen. The ball will then land in the receiver's court exactly the same way as the ball would in a real playground. Similarly, the stroke from B end is also measured, calculated and communicated to the computer at A end which releases a ball from the ball holder in the same manner as the ball would land in a physical match.

The ball boys in a virtual playground will have a lot more work to collect the balls and feed it to the ball holder very quickly. High resolution video and audio of both players will be displayed on a big screen at both ends so that the players can watch the stroke, expressions and movements. Umpires can watch the match from their home and playback and analyse the strokes, if required, and announce the results sitting at their home.

"What happened to Vini? Why is she not interested in watching tennis? She used to love watching tennis matches." Varad asked.

"Looks like she is not happy that I did not enthusiastically accept her idea. She is very moody. She will understand the realities and come out of her depression on her own. Not to worry." Vipul answered.

"Let me go and see her." Vijaya went in search of Vinitha.

xxx

Vinitha hated being dull and depressed. She was depressed not just because of the setback to her plans for begetting her child. She was more worried about the spread of Covid2121 and the increasing number of deaths. She got the news early in the morning that her close friend's mother died due to Covid2121. Her friend was inconsolable when she conveyed the news to Vinitha. Vinitha started getting very worried about her father and mother. She was very attached to them. She developed a nagging doubt that Covid2121 was not being handled properly. She kept telling people that Covid2121 was significantly different from Covid19 and the techniques used to control Covid19 are not going to be of help in controlling Covid2121. She could not explain her rationale, but she was sure that lockdown was not the solution for containing Covid2121. Apart from Covid2121, the mystery of the failed patch update from Robogenius was also troubling her. But she could not get any breakthrough in her investigation of the failed patch because Robogenius did not respond to her queries. She hated it when she was not able to move forward in her quest especially when it is in the national interest.

Vinitha searched in her cupboard for her 'moodinger'. She used the moodinger often to change her desolate mood to cheerful mood.

The moodinger is an electronic pad worn on the forehead and is controlled by a powerful computer inside the pad. The moodinger can store one's favourite situations in life and gives options to use several pre-set moods such as happiness, pleasant surprise, laughter, sober, etc. It also has options to mix the pre-recorded situations with pre-set moods, even custom develop uncommon moods. Using the combination of stored situations, pre-set moods and custom patterns, a moodinger can change the mood of the individual to the desired mood in minutes by interacting with the mind using neurotechnology.

Vinitha had carefully recorded and preserved her favourite situations including the occasion when her college principal announced her as the best outgoing student in the college, getting promotion within three months of joining her first job, getting the best employee award in the last office anniversary event, etc. She played back the pre-recorded incidents on the moodinger whenever she was depressed, often mixing the incidents with motivational pre-set moods.

Moodinger was banned in some countries due to protests from human rights organizations. There were reports that moodingers were used by terrorist organizations for brainwashing (brain training rather) new recruits in radical thoughts. Many countries have framed laws around 'Neuro Rights[1]' and there is clamour for bringing a stringent legal framework in India for 'Neuro Rights'. Indian government enacted a 'Neuro Rights' law but neuro rights activists are not happy with the tenacity of this law. Moodingers are increasingly used by police and investigation agencies as a lie detector test. Narco tests have been replaced by neurotechnology gadgets.

Vinitha took out the moodinger from its careful storage. A moodinger is very expensive and Vinitha treasured her moodinger. She had received it as an award in recognition of her contribution in a challenging security investigation. The moodinger came with various accessories, a pad to be worn around the forehead which extends and covers both the eyes with

---

[1] Neuro Rights - legal and ethical principles of freedom and entitlement related to an individual's cerebral or mental domain

a mini 3D display unit over the eyes, two tiny high-quality speakers as ear buds and connecting to the pad on the backside and a tiny tube-like structure hanging above the nostrils serving as smell sensor and smell generator.

Vinitha wore and adjusted all the paraphernalia and sat on the special chair given as part of the kit. She chose the event of getting the best outgoing student award and selected the pre-set mix of 'confidence' and closed her eyes and slowly removed all the negative thoughts from her mind. The moodinger would be able to give best results only when the mind is controlled and focused on the moodinger. The moodinger works best if the prerequisites are met. Vinitha had undertaken mind control training and exercises along with moodinger configuration and by now, perfected the art of getting the best results from the device.

Vijaya came to her room and saw that the room was locked from the inside. She peeped through the window and saw Vinitha sitting in a chair, eyes closed, wearing funny-looking accessories all over her face. Vinitha looked like a demon with all the wires and accessories on her face. Vijaya panicked seeing Vinitha and came running back to the living room.

Vinitha was used to the moodinger nowadays and got her mood transformed within five minutes. Earlier it used to take longer, sometimes even failure in the initial attempts. She could feel a faint smile escaping her lips within five minutes of switching on the moodinger. She removed the moodinger once she became cheerful.

Vijaya requested Vipul to go and find out what was troubling Vinitha. She was worried if it was the work of a bad ailment.

By the time Vipul came to her room, Vinitha had completed her moodinger session and opened the door using her remote. She was removing and packing her moodinger accessories. Vipul entered the room just then.

"Again, gone back to that stupid moodinger? You are going to get addicted to moodinger!" Vipul got irritated.

"What to do? I depend on a stupid device when my dear husband fails to cheer me. I also do not wish to depend on the device for the mood change but had to."

"You can chant *Vishnu Sahasranamam* and *Hanuman Chalisa*. They can cheer you up for sure in any situation. I do that. I don't depend on that stupid device."

"You can do that. I will not interfere. But I prefer my gadgets for my life."

Vipul said, "OK. I know you are upset that I did not enthusiastically agree with your plan. I thought about it, and I now agree to go with you on your plan."

It was a double bonanza for Vinitha. "I need not have used moodinger if only you had told me this half an hour ago. Anyway, better late than never."

"I am still scared but agree to go with you because you are very confident."

"Trust your wife. I thought about all the risks and built enough safeguards in my plan. Don't worry." Vinitha assured Vipul.

"Explain to me once again how you will remove the temporary license withdrawal?" Vipul asked.

"I saved the *hashing and salting*[2] of our license when it was issued to us. I stored it safely in my digital briefcase." Vinitha explained.

"I understand *hashing* but what is *salting?*" Vipul asked with genuine interest.

"Salting is the process of adding a unique value to the information so that a different hash value is created and thus difficult to reverse-engineer the hash value, normally used to store passwords." Vinitha explained.

"I remember the proverb in Tamil 'உப்பில்லாத பண்டம் குப்பையிலே'[3] You cyber security engineers are probably reengineering the proverb to 'உப்பில்லாத password reverse engineering binல'[4]" Vipul joked.

"Vinu, you just said that salting is done to protect from reverse engineering. But you are saying you will reverse engineer using hashing and salting. Are you not contradicting yourself?"

---

[2] Hashing and salting - Hashing is mapping data of any size to a fixed length using an algorithm so that integrity of the data is verified from the hash value. Salting is a unique value added to the password to create a different hash value so that it will be difficult to reverse engineer the hash value.

[3] Food items without salt to be dumped in the dustbin.

[4] Password without salt to be reverse-engineered.

"Because I am an ethical hacker[5]. I have access to multiple hashes and license and I can reverse engineer by deducing from multiple hashes."

"Anyway, the license has now been withdrawn. The old hash file would not make any sense." Vipul had his doubts.

"You may not know your wife's skills. But I am the best ethical hacker in the whole of India. My mind can think deeper than yours when it comes to hacking, ethical hacking."

"Explain it to me."

"I will reverse engineer from hashing and revert to the old status. Luckily, since we had the approved status for a brief time, I will be able to reverse engineer to that status. I will not be able to create a new status but I can put the status a step back."

"Did you not hear the official announcement? All the licenses approved after 14th April stand withdrawn. The government would have built an anomaly detection algorithm and will flag it as an alert if you manipulate the status, as the date of approval would still show Tuesday's date. They normally build AI algorithms to detect anomalies" Vipul was also an IT expert though not a cyber security expert.

---

[5] Ethical hacker - Practice of proactively detecting vulnerabilities in an application and/or IT infrastructure with the objective to fix the vulnerabilities before a hacker uses these vulnerabilities to hack.

"I thought about that. Again, lucky for us the government reversed the licenses only yesterday. We are late just by one day." Vinitha smiled.

"I cannot understand. It matters even if it is one day."

"I know how to put it back by one day."

"Not only the license date, but anomaly would also flag if the license date were older than the consultation date, even if it is by a day."

"I figured out everything. I will put back the consultation date also by a day."

"You will leave traces everywhere if you manipulate so many things."

"I know how to cover all my traces. If you remember, I did the Penetration Test for the Department of Health systems last month. My company got that prestigious assignment and I was the lead assessor for that project. I reviewed my penetration test records and I looked at the identified vulnerabilities. I checked the status of the systems online and three of the five major vulnerabilities still remain unaddressed. I can use these three vulnerabilities to alter the status and remove all the traces. They will not notice this manipulation now." Vinitha explained.

"Don't they have target to fix the identified vulnerabilities? Why do they commission Penetration Tests if they are not fixing the identified vulnerabilities?"

"Good question. They do have. The commitment is dependent on the severity of the risk. I know that the government has a policy of 'zero tolerance' for procrastination with respect to cyber security. Our Prime Minister is very particular about this. Government fixed 72 hours as the Service Level Commitment to fix all 'Critical' vulnerabilities. The government formed a separate department within the 'Ministry of Cyber Security' to monitor this. The Health Department missed this time probably because of the work pressure from Covid2121 situation. This costly miss has become handy for us now" Vinitha explained.

"I am still not clear. Assuming the three vulnerabilities still exist in the system, how would that help you to reverse-engineer and clear all the traces"

"Let me be specific. Tell me if you can understand. I will explain in simple language. I am going to do 'Horizontal privilege escalation attack' exploiting one of the vulnerabilities identified by me. Since the vulnerability was identified by me and I have all the details about this vulnerability, I will be able to perform 'privilege escalation attack'" Vinitha smiled. But looking at Vipul's puzzled face, she continued.

"Horizontal privilege escalation attack is gaining access to a valid login account and then bypassing authorization channel, and successfully gaining access to the administrative privilege. Anything can be done once administrative privilege is gained"

"I don't think it is still going to be that easy. They would have built multiple checks and balances." Vipul was still worried.

"I checked all the security mechanisms as I still retain high security credentials for all the health applications including the application which released our license."

"Assuming you manage to do this, you will become an **Unethical Hacker** and not **an Ethical Hacker.**"

"No. *White Hat hacker to Grey Hat Hacker but not Black Hat*[6]. Does not matter? I am conscious that this is my right, and I am doing this only to enforce my right. My hacking may be questionable, but my ethics are not."

"Meaning?" still doubtful Vipul. "I believe it is unethical to tamper with my basic right of childbirth. So, I am going to use my ethical hacking skills to counter this unethical act." Vipul was hesitant, but he knew when to accept defeat.

xxx

By the time Vinitha and Vipul came to the living room, the Wimbledon match was over and *Abra* was switched off. Varad and Vijaya were happy seeing Vinitha in a cheerful mood. They were not sure what made her to change her mood.

"Let us finish dinner early today." Vinitha announced.

---

[6] White, Black & Grey Hat Hacker - White hat hackers probe cybersecurity weaknesses to develop stronger security; black hat hackers are motivated by malicious intent; and Gray hat hackers not malicious, but they're not always ethical

"Both of us would like to skip the dinner, Vinu." Varad replied. Sevugan came with a plate and two glasses and gave it to Varad and Vijaya.

"What is that special for you?" Vinitha asked.

"*Panankalkandu pal*[7] for both of us. We take milk every night. I informed Sevugan to make it a daily practice and he is giving us the milk every day on the dot, sharp on time without fail. Good boy!" Varad appreciated.

Vinitha gave an undefinable expression. A Vinitha speciality that no one can interpret. Or perhaps, each interprets it the way they want it.

Vinitha's phone rang and she answered the call in public mode. All calls have the option of public mode as well as private mode. If answered in public mode, video and audio come up on the *Abra* wall screen.

Vinitha's colleague, Vanaja, came on the screen. "Vinitha, I have an update for the information you asked about Robogenius OS." Vanaja was close to Vinitha in age but reported to Vinitha. She was shorter and slightly more filled than Vinitha and hence looked older than her. Vinitha had risen very quickly in the hierarchy because of her strong performance. Though Vanaja was her subordinate, Vinitha treated her more as a friend than a subordinate. Vinitha had developed the habit of being friendly with all her subordinates, especially performing subordinates.

---

[7] Panankalkandu pal - Palm candy milk

Vanaja was not jealous of Vinitha's fast growth and had expressed her preference to work in Vinitha's team not least because of this character of Vinitha. Vinitha was also known for her fairness though she was a taskmaster. Vinitha and Vanaja were known as 'Victorious Vs' in office.

"Excellent. Shoot."

"The bug reported on Robotma v7.4.1 is apparently a *Denial-of-Service* attack."

"Denial of service attack? I cannot believe it. V7.4.1 was released to fix the *Remote Code Execution* vulnerability. How can the version released to fix a vulnerability create another vulnerability? Strange and unbelievable."

"What is Denial of Service?" Vipul asked.

"Technique used by the attackers to stop or slow down a service by flooding the service with requests." This time it was Vanaja from the screen. Vanaja was a good trainer apart from being a good cyber forensic expert in her company.

"Did you check if v7.4.0 had a denial-of-service vulnerability?

"I checked. But there was no report that v7.4.0 had or was having denial of service vulnerability. We are still using v7.4.0 but there are no reports coming of denial of service even now."

"Did you check with anyone who reported the bug? Unfortunately, my husband never upgraded the patch to v7.4.1

and hence I could not check the details in our robot." Vinitha asked.

"I will check with all our staff whether anyone used v7.4.1 and get back to you," saying this Vanaja disconnected the call.

Abra switched on the flashing red light when Sevugan was serving the glasses to Varad and Vijaya. Sevugan dropped the glass on the floor because of the shock of the sudden red light and sound.

"Don't you understand that it is an alert message? A flashing red alert is an everyday affair nowadays and you see and hear it almost every day. I thought you are an intelligent robot." Vinitha cribbed.

"Madam, this has nothing to do with intelligence. This is called involuntary action. Involuntary actions in a human like you are controlled by *medulla oblongata* whereas voluntary actions are controlled by *cerebrum*. All actions are controlled by the same CPU in robots like us though we have high power parallel processors. Hence, our response will be different from that of humans for involuntary actions." Sevugan explained.

Vinitha was not impressed. "You have learnt to react well to everything", "involuntarily" she added after a couple of seconds.

Meanwhile *Abra* started reading the red alert breaking news. It was a message from the Health Secretary to the Government of India who started reading out from a paper from his office room.

The picture of Prime Minister Ashok Raj could be seen in the background.

"Covid2121 is spreading fast. The government is managing to control the impact of the deadly disease with the guidance of the Honourable Prime Minister." He then started quoting some statistics comparing the number of active infected patients, number of reported deaths, total population, etc., of India, compared with that of a few other countries like USA, China and Australia to prove his point that India was doing better than other countries. The irony was that there was a press statement by the Leader of Opposition quoting some similar statistics to say that India was worse affected by Covid2121 compared to USA, China and Australia.

He finished his *gyan* with the message:

"The Honourable Prime Minister is requesting all citizens to cooperate with the government to contain the spread. Stay indoors. Do not walk out of the house even for exercise unless you have the necessary permission for the same. The government has instructed the police department to be strict and arrest even walkers, retail vendors, etc. All shops including that of street vendors have been asked to close and migrate to online sales. Please procure all your requirements online. Remember to choose only those online companies who use 100% robots for deliveries. There were some reports that the spread is increasing through human delivery agents and hence the government has ordered all online retailers to use only robots for deliveries. Check if your favourite online retailer is using robots for delivery before placing your order."

"This is unfair. How can they just announce new rules daily? Today they are banning all human delivery agents because of Covid. Did they think of the long-term impact of such acts?" Vinitha was furious.

"It seems to be a sensible suggestion Vinu, why are you getting wild? It is simple logic. The government brought in a lockdown to reduce Covid. Lockdown is not controlling Covid spread. They then started looking at other avenues to limit human-to-human interaction. One area left was the possible interaction with the delivery agents if they are human. Robots will not get impacted by Covid." Vipul explained.

"It is unfair. You cannot control everything through ordinances." Vinitha countered.

"Where is the question of unfairness in this? We know that robots will get involved more and more in life threatening actions. The Indian Army has already got two strong robot battalions, and they are the first to be used in insurgency actions. They are more effective than humans. Robots have replaced humans in bomb disposal squads" Vipul answered.

"It is still unfair. They are doing all these because robots will not protest, and robots do not have voting power. If robots get voting power, they cannot afford to bring such Acts." Vinitha would not agree that easily.

"I agree with madam. I am going to ask our association to include in their charter of demands 'to ban robots being used for menial and life-threatening jobs'." Sevugan added.

"Who will do these jobs then? How will you survive lockdown if robots are not to be used for delivery? Even you need your essentials to be procured." Vipul asked.

"That is not my problem. I don't need to answer that question. Maybe, humans will invent one more breed of machines with limited or no intelligence. We are intelligent robots, and we should be treated well." Sevugan protested.

"As a Prime Minister of a country such as India looked at by every other country for solutions, it is his responsibility to try all possible options to resolve this virus problem. I don't find anything wrong with this move. You are blaming the government now. You will blame the government even more vociferously if you later found out that the virus spread was due to human delivery agents".

"I will not. How will the government protect the livelihood of the human delivery agents? How will their families survive especially during the gruelling lockdown?" Vinitha diverted the discussion topic knowing well that she should not have started the discussion about robots in the presence of Sevugan.

"That is their problem. They should have enhanced their skills. The government gave equal education opportunities to every citizen. The government cannot guarantee a job for every citizen.

The government can only enable opportunities." Vipul put forth his point strongly.

"My dear husband, that is not how society works. Remember India is still a 'socialist, secular, democratic republic' as per our Constitution."

"Who cares? That was framed in 1947. We are in the 22nd century now. The world is changing. We must move forward."

"It is not the …ism that matters. It is the implementation that matters. Why do we fight for some stupid fools in politics? No more discussion on this." Varad switched off *Abra* and the lights.

As predicted by Vinitha, breaking news for the next morning was: "Government of India promulgates an ordinance overnight banning the use of humans as delivery agents." The ordinance was signed by the President of India at 12:01AM. That signature in the middle of the night sounded the death knell for some 15 logistics companies that had not modernized their workforce.

Spokespersons of the ruling party in online debates quoted the famous quote by Confucius: *"There is only one thing in life which never changes and that is change. All companies should keep themselves adaptable to the technology changes."*

MONDAY, 21ST APRIL 2121

Vipul could not afford to laze in bed the next day because he had a very important *shadverse* conference at 9.30 AM. That was the project kick-off meeting scheduled by Vipul's company and he had an important role in that as Project Manager for South Zone implementation. Vipul got up at the first alarm message from *Abra*. *Abra* still continued to play the uninvited prefix Covid2121 warning message.

Vipul was very happy and motivated to take up that important role as this was a nationally important project. There could be lots of challenges but lots of learnings as well. Vipul always saw the positive aspects of new assignments.

Project Director, Ankur kicked off the meeting by explaining the importance of the project with its background, scope of their work and the critical success factors for the project. He took pains to first explain the need for the project.

Ever since India overtook USA as the largest economy in the world, the government had introduced lots of amendments tightening visa norms and citizenship conditions in India. There was a growing interest from some citizens of developing countries to get Indian citizenship and settle in India. The present government introduced amendments to tighten immigration permissions and work visas to India with the objective to reduce illegal immigration to India, but the problem continued. This had become a big problem and a potential embarrassment to the government.

He further explained the problems faced by the country in controlling illegal immigration. Porous borders with the neighbouring countries were a big problem in controlling 'illegal immigration' to India. Visa seekers to India normally preferred to take the route through the neighbouring countries as its borders were long and porous. Improvements in flyo technology were posing a big problem for the Border Security Force. Specially built flyos were used by the illegal immigrants to deceive the prying eyes of air surveillance as they deceive air surveillance radars at the borders. Illegal immigration rackets to get entry into India were popular around the world. They sold it as a package including entry to Nepal or Bangladesh and then illegal entry in a flyo through one of the less scrutinized entry points. These flyos dropped the passengers deep inside the Indian border. Premium packages include settling them in India and getting the necessary digital identifications for them.

The Prime Minister of India proposed Digital Walls along the entire border with Pakistan, Nepal and Bangladesh to stop illegal immigration. The digital wall was an important promise in his election manifesto in the last parliamentary election. Digital wall is an air surveillance network along India's borders using a powerful radar network that can detect and shoot flyos and other flying objects crossing the wall without a valid visa uploaded on their license file. Visa had to be activated in the flyo's license for anyone to cross the border legally into India using a flyo. The radar network would automatically scan and detect visa stamping in the flyos and bring down any vehicle entering without a valid visa stamping. Once the digital wall is built along the entire border, it would be impossible to penetrate illegally through air. Ankit stopped his long introductory speech.

Ankit added, "Our company received the prestigious order from the Government of India to build digital walls for about 5000 kms of our borders. We received the contract signed by the Government of India last week and this is a landmark project for us. We have a lot at stake in this project and that is why we selected very capable project managers for this project."

One of the project managers who was pessimistic about the project quipped, "Is it possible to build a digital wall for such a long and treacherous terrain? Is it a good idea?"

"The Prime Minister has done detailed diligence, and this is his favourite project. He is very optimistic about it. What is your problem? How could you lead the project if you start with doubts?" Ankit asked instantly.

"I am not pessimistic. I read from history that a US President by the name of Donald Trump started a project for building a wall along USA and Mexico border which failed miserably, and he lost his next election. I was reminded of this."

"Our Honourable Prime Minister Ashok Raj is not Donald Trump and he knows how to make this project succeed. He will not start anything which is likely to fail. And this is not your problem. Don't start any initiative with nagging doubts."

The project manager did not open his mouth after that.

Vipul was not sure if he should ask but asked, "I understand the threat from the neighbouring countries along the northern borders. But what is my role as South Zone Project Manager? We have only a coastline as the border in the south."

Ankit replied, "Good question Vipul. That is the power of vision of our Prime Minister. He does not plan anything in half measure. He wants to build a digital wall along the entire coastline as well though the priority is for the land borders. This project will mainly kick-start in Phase 2. But the digital wall along the entire Tamil Nadu coastline will come up in Phase 1 itself, as there is a threat from Sri Lanka as well. Remember, flyos can travel from Sri Lanka to India. Moreover, digital walls will take care of illegal immigrations via boats and ships as well."

The meeting took about 80 minutes as a project plan was worked out and agreed to by all the Project Managers.

Vipul asked towards the end of the meeting, "Building a digital wall would require onsite work. We cannot build a digital wall by working from home. Why are we kick-starting the project in the middle of Covid2121 lockdown?"

"The government has given special permission for onsite work for this project as this is Prime Minister's favourite project. All of you will get a Covid2121 permit to travel and a car from the company with a Covid2121 license." Agarwal replied.

Vipul thought to himself, "Approved child license is cancelled because of Covid2121 but digital wall project can progress as usual. Strange priorities."

Ankit asked, "Do you have any more questions, Vipul?"

"No sir. Nothing." Vipul quickly replied.

When Vipul was getting briefed by Ankit about this exciting project, Vinitha also received interesting information about her ongoing cyber investigation. She was raring to share the update with Vipul. She was waiting for Vipul to complete and kept peeping into the study room very often.

Vanaja had sent a message to Vinitha giving the details she had asked for and the message had the option 'Click here to call Vanaja back'. The message was very interesting and aroused Vinitha's curiosity. Vinitha pressed the call back button. A video call was connected to Vanaja immediately.

"I sent you all the details I could get, Vinitha." Vanaja came on the screen with a big smile.

"Thank You Vanaja for the quick response. That is what makes us a great combination. Let me understand your message. You mentioned that 26 of our staff use NGN robots supplied by Robogenius. How sure are you about this number? How did you get this number so fast?"

"Simple Vinitha. Our HRMS[1] database has this information. I asked our HR head, and he gave me this info."

"Why are we capturing info about house robots in HRMS?"

"Do you remember our management announced a new benefit for all the employees a couple of months back - that the company would sponsor Robotcare insurance for all the employees? Robotcare insurance takes care of all service and maintenance expenses for the house robots. Our HR head later clarified that Robotcare would be taken only for NGN robots as the premiums for older generation robots were found to be very high. So, HR ran a survey in our HRMS and collected all the necessary information about the house robots of all the employees. My job became very simple." Vanaja smiled.

"That is good anyway. You then found out that only eight employees out of these 26 upgraded to Robotma v7.4.1. That is a very poor percentage. We are a cyber security company and only

---

[1] HRMS – Human Resources Management System

30% of our employees follow our advice. I shall inform our CEO to first *put our own house in order*." Vinitha smiled.

"How did you find this info? Is the patch version also captured in our HRMS? That would be very cumbersome."

"No. Not in HRMS. I sent a chat message to all the 26 employees in our internal 'Org Chat' tool and got the response back from all these 26 employees."

"Good. But the next piece of information is intriguing. You are saying that only two out of these eight had problems when running with v7.4.1. Are you sure about this? Are you sure that they understood your chat message properly? Because this piece of info does not sound correct to me".

"I am 100% sure madam. Once I got the chat response from all 26, I made a call to all eight who used v7.4.1. I explained to them over the phone and got the confirmation from them." Vanaja switched to calling Vinitha madam at times.

"Very interesting. We need to go deeper into this aspect. If the OS is buggy, why would it affect only two robots out of the eight robots running the same buggy OS? This does not sound logical to me".

"Could it be possible that only two of the eight were attacked for the Denial of Service. It is not necessary that all eight would get attacked."

"True, but it does not look like an attack. If it is an attack, the Robogenius team would have found out the vulnerability and fixed it rather than withdraw the version."

"I am not able to think madam, you do the thinking. I'll do the action part. Tell me what to do further."

Vipul and Varad joined her by then.

"Did you check with the two reported employees to find out when did they face the problem and did they report to anyone?"

"I did that Vinitha" Vanaja was very happy that she did something without asking. "Both of them had configured for auto-update and hence the version got updated automatically when the new version was released. They **noticed the problem from the time the new version got updated**"

"What did they notice? Did they report to anyone?"

"Incidentally, both gave the same response. Their robots became very tired, disobeyed all their instructions and behaved like a diseased and old human" Vanaja was always thorough and systematic in her investigative work.

"Exactly like me. So, it is possible to make the robots senile and sick" Varad interrupted.

"And they became normal only after downgrading to the old version" Vanaja finished.

"Interesting. Why would the robots going slow be reported as 'Denial of Service' attack? This does not look like the behaviour of 'Denial of Service' attack".

"Denial of Service makes the service unavailable or slows down the service. That is why." Vanaja could not complete the sentence.

"I have a rationale Vanaja, for my statement. **Firstly, an attacker has to execute 'Denial of Service' attack. Why would the impact be noticed as soon as the version was upgraded as if an attacker was watching for them to complete the upgrade to start the attack immediately?** Does not sound logical to me" Vinitha explained.

"Vinitha. I get your point. Do you mean to say Robogenius, such a big enterprise, did not understand this simple fact? They must have analyzed the logs"

"True. But for some strange reason, Robogenius is keeping mum. Robogenius must very well be aware that it is not a 'Denial of Service' attack. But they are not denying because it suits them. They are worried about something more damaging and hence are playing along the theory of 'Denial of Service' attack"

"I cannot believe" Vipul retorted.

"You are talking complex. 'Remote Code Execution' has now become 'Denial of Service'. My only concern is on Sevugan running around with a gun in his hand and you guys are not doing anything about that" Varad went back to his gun theory, rather worry.

"What do you want me to do, Vinitha?" Vanaja asked.

"OK. Leave it to me for now. Let me think about it. Send me those eight names. I will speak to them and find out if I can get more information. I specifically want to find differences between the two who got affected and the other six who did not feel the impact even after upgrading to the new version Are your sure the other six used v7.4.1 but did not notice the issue"

"100%. Four of the other six are still running with v7.4.1 and their robots are working perfectly normal"

"Good information. It is my job now" Vinitha disconnected the call without logically closing the call. She did this often when she got into deep thinking. But people like Vanaja did not mind her brusqueness because they knew her well.

-x-x-

Vipul as well as Vinitha were in an upbeat mood for the rest of the day.

Sevugan came to Vipul's office room. After ensuring that Vinitha was not anywhere near, Sevugan asked, "Master, I need some advice and I don't want madam to know about this."

Vipul was worried about continuing the discussion in the absence of Vinitha. He thought of Vinitha's warnings about

Sevugan, and quipped uninterestingly, "Sevugan, you are intelligent. What can I advise you that you would not know?"

"Thanks master. I am asked for advice by a fellow robot and I don't have any knowledge or experience in this and that is why I am asking you."

Vipul was a little relaxed. He took his attention away from his laptop and said, "Go on. Shoot."

"One of our fellow robots in the association is asked by her master to marry her. She is asking my advice. What do I tell her?"

"The government has legalized human-to-robot marriage recently. The Supreme Court allowed human-to-robot marriage in a plaint by an activist and the government approved the Act in the parliament against opposition from right-wing members."

"So, this is legally allowed now. I read it on the Internet but would like to confirm it with you." Sevugan said.

"Yes, but with a lot of conditions. The government did not want to displease the protestors and hence put in a lot of conditions."

"Like?"

"Both the parties need to apply and get the sanction from the Registrar of Marriages. Marriages without approval will be deemed illegal."

"I cannot understand why a human would partner with a robot. Unimaginable."

"That is psychology and it is difficult for a robot to understand human psychology."

"That is OK. But we cannot believe humans. They may change their mind and start harassing their partners. What legal protection do we have?"

"The Act gives a lot of protection to the robot partner, for example, the human partner can be arrested without any investigation if the robot partner makes a complaint with the robot police. That is the highlight of this Act. I do not remember all the clauses, though. I will give you a copy of the Act. You can go through it."

Sevugan said, "That is very fair," and went away.

-x-x-

Vipul was upbeat and shared with the family at the lunch table about his role in the digital wall project. They got to have lunch together because both Vipul and Vinitha were working from home.

"I think this idea of a digital wall is not required in our current context." Varad commented.

"Why are you saying this uncle? Many ideas initiated by our PM looked ridiculous in the beginning, but we are seeing the results. India is making rapid progress in the last 20 years. Our Prime Minister is a visionary. Every country is acknowledging our progress. The world looks up to our Prime Minister as a master statesman. What matters at the end of the day is economic progress." Vipul remembered his project director's speech.

"Economic progress at what cost? Do you know that we are sliding down even more rapidly in the ranking of democracy amongst other countries in the globe? India is pushed to 118th rank in the democracy index. India goes to elections and selects its representatives. But the elections are only symbolic. The ruling party is so powerful and is in power for the past 20 years. With a strong majority, they have systematically clipped the powers of all the constitutional authorities. It is very easy to enact new laws to their advantage." Vinitha started the argument.

"Development is more important. Who cares about democracy? They are winning the elections again and again. People vote for them. A large cross-section of the people do not bother to question the government. The balance is not interested to oppose for fear of intimidation." Vipul justified.

"Vinitha is correct, *mapillai*, in a way. India was not a superpower during our times, but we were happier then compared to now," said Varad. He thought 'his time' ended when he turned 60.

"You are not happy because of your illness. How is a democracy or lack of democracy affecting it? If people are not happy, why are they repeatedly voting for this government?" Vipul questioned.

"Because of various reasons. This government is very good at brand marketing. They create an illusion that is difficult to beat. Even educated people like you are falling prey to their misinformation campaign. But 'freedom of expression' and privacy are more important to me than my economic status. Strikes have been banned across the country. Participating in strikes is treated as treason, working against the interests of the country. If someone hears our discussion, I could be put behind bars on charges of 'threat to national security'. That is our sorry situation."

"Why are you arguing that we don't have freedom of expression? We have free press, free media. Government does not own and control media"

"You are not aware Vipul. Government indirectly owns media. All media companies have been acquired by corporates friendly to the government. You will not see any anti-government news"

"Assume it is true, it is not illegal for a corporate to acquire a media company. Every party has the same choice. What is the problem here?"

"It is not illegal, but it is stifling free expression. Press is considered 'fourth estate' in our democracy. That could be one reason we are sliding down on democracy index"

"Vinitha, I agree that we are sliding down on democracy and 'freedom of expression' to individuals. But look at our political history. Many countries progressed only when an authoritarian was at the helm of affairs. Ashok Raj is a confirmed authoritarian. He means business and you can do business in India only if you are an authoritarian." Vipul brought a new dimension to the discussion. "Only an authoritarian leader can bring in order and growth."

"No, which country are you talking about?" Vinitha did not want to give up.

"Singapore. Singapore was never a great democracy. Lee Kwan Yew was a very popular world leader and highly revered not only in Singapore, but across the world. But he was perceived as an authoritarian. Strikes were banned in Singapore for centuries. Singapore never enjoyed the freedom of press in real terms. But how does all this matter? Singaporeans are happy with their government and they continue to vote for Lee's progeny. They never stopped growing." Vipul explained.

"Singapore is to be viewed from a different perspective. You cannot make a generalized inference that authoritarians can only bring in development and earn respect. What about Winston Churchill and Abraham Lincoln? They were consensual leaders and could develop their respective countries." Vinitha never gave up and that too when arguing with Vipul.

"What about China? There was a popular leader in China, Xi Jinping. He was credited to have brought economic progress to China. All the developed countries used to be afraid of China during his reign. He was known to be an authoritarian." Vipul would also not give up easily.

"Mahatma Gandhi was the most loved and most respected leader in our own history. He never took up any government position. He never succumbed to the pleasures of brand marketing. He was consensual. Leaders would be of different traits. We cannot generalize based on one or two individuals." Vinitha used her *Brahmastra*.

Vipul did not want to continue the argument and hence left it at that. "I will stop supporting the government the moment our people stop voting for them." Vipul concluded his side of the argument. At least, he thought he did.

"Only if you stop voting for them will the government change. So, there is no logic in this stand. Anyway, you then have to wait for a long time. They are surviving for long because of multiple reasons and lack of a strong alternative is one reason." Vinitha concluded and got up from the dining table.

Vipul started the discussion on Sevugan's doubt about robot-human marriage. He wanted to divert the attention away from the political debate which invariably ended up in a heated argument between them. Luckily Varad got excited and picked up the new discussion.

Varad vehemently opposed the move to legalize human-robot marriages, whereas Vipul was pointing out that many countries had already legalized it.

"It is OK for others but not for us. India is known for a very strong cultural heritage." Varad opined.

"How would legalizing a marriage with a robot go against the cultural heritage?" asked Vipul.

Vinitha was getting irritated with their argument. "How does this matter to us? Are you in love with any robot? If so, tell me. I will give you a divorce."

"No. No. Just from a logical point of view. Why should I, when I have a lovable and intelligent human wife?" Vipul smiled "who argues with me vehemently very often" quickly added. Vinitha and Varad laughed aloud and the stress there disappeared.

"We are wasting our time in stupid arguments and not bothering about important things. Let me check the status of the Robotma patch upgrade." Vinitha sounded irritated visibly.

"*Abra*, tell me the hot news about Robogenius." Vinitha ordered.

"Robogenius released the corrected version of the patch to their Robotma OS v7.4.1 yesterday. As per reports from the industry, the new version is running smoothly without any reported issue, so far. Robogenius has not disclosed the reason for the failure of the earlier release. Our efforts to reach the CEO of Robogenius, Mr. Vinod Sharma, did not yield any result."

"That is too bad. They seemed to have released the patch yesterday, but we were not aware. How come?" Vinitha was surprised.

"Both of us were busy from early morning today. We missed the Morning News update and retired early yesterday. They seem to have released it late in the evening yesterday and this news is of medium priority alert. Only high priority alerts and red alerts are notified on the phone." Vipul explained.

"So, Robogenius fixed the remote code execution vulnerability with Sevugan? He will no longer run around with a gun in his hand." Varad was always worried about a gun-toting robot.

"There is no information about fixing the vulnerability in the news update. I need to check the release notes of yesterday's release."

"Vinu, shall I upgrade Sevugan to the new version 7.4.1?" Vipul asked. He remembered her warning about not upgrading to new patches quickly.

"Don't do it yet. Let me first check the release notes. Also, I asked my office to create a honeypot. Let us run a honeypot with the vulnerable version for a couple of days before upgrading to the clean version."

"You are confusing me. It is difficult to understand you." Vipul expressed his disappointment.

"Does not matter. Do as I say."

"What is a honeypot?" Vipul queried.

"Honeypot is a virtual trap to lure the attackers surreptitiously so that useful information can be collected about the attackers and attack." Vinitha explained.

"You could have said in one word *mousetrap*, so Sevugan is going to be the *masala vadai* in your honeypot" Vipul joked.

"Don't worry. I will ensure that no harm will come to your friend Sevugan." Vinitha teased him back.

"Vinu, also ensure that nothing happens to us by keeping Sevugan vulnerable longer." Varad intervened.

"No worries appa. Only for a very short time."

Just then, *Abra* sounded the red alarm. Vipul could not ask any more question.

A man with a salt and pepper beard, bespectacled, nearly bald, typical scientist look, came on the screen and started taking lessons about Covid2121, the structure of the virus, how the virus spreads from human to human, how the virus spreads inside our body and how a virus is treated. He explained the precautions to be taken to contain the virus. He insisted that people wear masks even when inside their homes. He explained the difference between the masks used daily when traveling on the city roads and the masks to be used to contain Covid2121. Masks are to be used on a daily basis, but these masks were of filtering type to filter pollutants and harmful gases. Covid2121 virus can get through these filters. Covid2121 masks are built such that they can block the virus. The scientist explained.

"He is the top virologist in the country, Dr. Vittal Lobo. A globally respected virologist. He is very busy nowadays giving interviews on an hourly basis." Vipul explained to others.

"Please stock sufficient number of Covid2121 masks for use. We recommend that you use masks all the time even when you are at home." Vittal beamed on the screen.

The scientist vanished from the screen and a reporter started reading old reports about the dreaded Covid19 virus, how it was claimed to have started from a sea food market in a town known as Wuhan in China of the olden days. (ShenZhi is supposed to be the erstwhile Wuhan) and how it spread across the globe, how countries were unprepared for the four waves of Covid2019, etc. The reporter closed the report with a statement - "The origin of Covid19 is still a mystery, even after 100 years. There were some unverified reports that the virus originated from a lab in Wuhan. It remains inconclusive and a mystery even now."

"It will remain a mystery even after 1000 years. Governments know the source, but they are afraid of revealing it." Varad quoted.

"It is getting messy. Going by the studies, I don't think this is going to die down in 2121. I heard that it took five years for the world to come to terms with Covid2019." Vipul said.

"I read a report in a USA news channel that the scientists are wrong in their analysis that Covid2121 spreads by human-human contact. All the analytical models predicted that five days of stringent lockdown should have brought down the doubling rate. But we are seeing the R curve going steeply upward. This does not appear to be spread by humans." Vinitha said.

"What does Dr. Vittal say about this?" Vipul asked.

"He is non-committal. He says it is possible. They still don't have clear clues on how the virus spreads despite a lockdown. They are apparently looking at all possibilities including animal-human contacts."

"We should note that it took more than two months to bring down the spread in the case of Covid19 in spite of a lockdown. It takes time. Why are we in such a hurry to cast aspersions, we are only in the 5th day of lockdown?" Vipul asked.

"Effectiveness of the current lockdown cannot be compared with the lockdown during 2020. With the advancement in technology and strict lockdown measures imposed, the current lockdown is much more effective than the one 100 years ago. Analytics models take the previous numbers into consideration and predict that the R curve should have come down to one by now. Nobody knows the reason for the failure of the models. No clue."

"I don't know when this is going to end. I am now more determined to go ahead with my plans." Vinitha sounded more stubborn when she said that.

"Your plans of changing your hat from white to grey" Vipul added and smiled.

TUESDAY, 22ND APRIL 2121

The day started with a very interesting finding but ended disastrously.

Vanaja logged into Sevugan remotely and installed the honeypot early in the morning. Vinitha was impressed by her commitment.

But she called back worriedly, "Vinitha, I installed the honeypot code in Sevugan, but the honeypot does not seem to be active."

"Why do you say that?"

"I injected attack simulation in Sevugan to test the effectiveness of the honeypot but the honeypot is not responding at all."

"Funny. Are you sure the honeypot code is good to go? Did you check with multiple robots before installing it in Sevugan?"

"Yes, Vinitha. I checked in a minimum of five Robogenius robots. They all responded to the same simulation."

"And all of them were running Robotma v7.4.0?"

"Yes, Vinitha."

"One possibility, Vanaja, is that Sevugan has already been attacked."

"Is it possible? But you said Sevugan is not displaying any signs of being the victim of an attack!"

"You know Vanaja, malicious code would stay resident for a longer time collecting and sending data surreptitiously. Could be an *Advance Persistent Attack*[1]"

"But I ran malware scanning thoroughly in Sevugan. Not one but multiple scans. None of the scans detected anything suspicious."

"That is a valid point. That is what I would also do immediately. But that does not rule out the possibility of an attack. This attack vector must have escaped all known malware scanning tools."

"Yes, possible. What do we do now?"

"It is possible that Sevugan has already been attacked and is silently sending sensitive information to a **'Command & Control Server**[2]**'.**"

---

[1] An Advanced Persistent Threat (APT) is an attack campaign in which an intruder establishes an illicit, long-term presence on a network in order to mine highly sensitive data

[2] Command & Control Server - Computer controlled by an attacker which sends commands to systems compromised to control them or get sensitive data from them.

"You would have already hardened Sevugan and I can easily check if Sevugan is sending information to any malicious IP by analysing the traffic logs and also by initiating a *sniffer*[3]." Vanaja offered.

"Let us do that."

After analysing the logs for the past week, Vinitha and Vanaja decided that Sevugan was not sending message to any Command & Control Server.

"We got to some interesting leads, but all the leads are hitting roadblocks." Vinitha started putting all the leads and inferences as a *mind map*[4].

Varad came running to her before she could complete the mind map and informed her that her mother was still in bed which was unusual. Vinitha checked the temperature using a digital thermometer.

The thermometer announced, "Normal temperature for the human body is 98.4°F and the temperature is now showing 100.2°F. An increase in temperature could be due to various reasons. However, it is strongly recommended that you take an RTPCR test to know if this fever is due to Covid2121. I must tell you that this temperature reading has been sent to the Central Health Database automatically."

---

[3] sniffer – A software tool that enables "sniffing" or monitoring network traffic in real-time to analyse.

[4] mind map – Pictorial representation of thoughts in a logical sequence.

Vinitha got frustrated and switched off the thermometer. "Nowadays everything starting from the tutor to a computer, a broom to a cream, is advising us. I did not realize that this temperature reading would also be sent to Health Database. That is atrocious."

Vijaya's temperature was high but she did not cough and there were no symptoms of a cold. Though there were repeated announcements asking everyone to test for Covid2121 for any symptoms including fever, cold, cough, etc., Vinitha did not opt to test as she was sure that her mother could not have gotten infected with Covid2121. Vinitha's parents were quarantined in a separate room ever since they came down to Chennai. They did not step out of the house. Neither did they meet any visitor at home. The only people they interacted with were Vipul, Vinitha and Sevugan, of course. None of the other three, including Sevugan, showed any signs of infection and there was no reason for anyone in this house to get Covid infection. Vinitha was very careful with her parents as she was paranoid about their co-morbidity.

Vinitha finally agreed to do a RTPCR test at home at the insistence of Vipul. Vipul said, "Nothing wrong with testing, Vinu. We will know for sure, and we can be free after that."

She ordered a test only for her mother as she was confident that her fever should be due to the common cold and not Covid2121.

The test result came in as a phone message within two hours and all of them were shocked at seeing the test report. They started panicking. The test report had come as Covid2121 positive.

"How could my mother be positive? We avoided all possible contact for her. This must be false positive." Vinitha was very upset. She was very careful that her parents should not get the infection and still it happened. She could not accept her defeat easily.

"It is very rare to be false positive. We cannot take it lightly. Would it be possible that they got infected before they left Madurai, possibly at the hospital?" Vipul suggested a possible explanation.

"Not possible. It is six days since they left Madurai. If they had gotten infected at Madurai, the symptoms would have shown within three days as per Covid2121 behaviour. I searched on the Internet and got to understand everything about Covid2121. Covid2121 behaviour is not the same as that of Covid19." Vinitha said.

"Could be possible that it is delayed symptom in her case, as it is showing up after five days?"

"Not possible. I read reports that Covid2121 shows symptoms within three days of infection. Asymptomatic is possible but symptomatic shows up within three days." Vinitha had taken a keen interest in reading about Covid2121 ever since she brought them home as she was worried about the possibility of them getting infected. Her natural inclination to delve deep into any problem and solution-finding approach convinced Vipul about the veracity of her statement. He didn't doubt her statement.

Vinitha made all arrangements to admit her mother in a private hospital. The hospital sent a special ambulance with Covid2121 protected staff and picked up the patient themselves.

"Can I come with her?" Vinitha asked.

"No. You can accompany or visit amma only if you show a positive RTPCR test report. Otherwise, none of you would be allowed to see or meet her. But not to worry, we will take care of everything and will send periodic updates to both of your phones. We now have a *shadverse* option in the Covid2121 room and you can have a chat with amma in *shadverse*." The ambulance staff said politely and left with Vijaya.

"She must have picked up the virus in Chennai only. Who all came to our house?" Vinitha started her investigation process right after seeing the ambulance off.

"We did not receive any guest. There were only a few delivery vendors and many of them were robots, we can eliminate robots as a possible source of infection. But all the vendors came home fully protected and we did not allow them to come anywhere near your parents. We did not go anywhere in the last five days. I collected materials from the vendors and I used a mask, anti-infection surgical gloves before receiving materials from the delivery vendors. Since your parents are here, I was extremely careful so much so that I removed my mask only in the bathroom for the past three days." Vipul tried to lighten the moment but could not.

"Could it be possible that one of us picked up the infection asymptomatically and passed it to your mother?" Vipul thought about the possibility.

"Possible. That is the only possibility. We will come to know if we test all of us." Vinitha answered.

"Anyway, let us now test for all of us." Vipul was always cautious.

"Makes sense." Vinitha ordered home sample pickup for all of them.

All the test reports came Covid negative within three hours.

"Very strange. Let us do a '**Root Cause Analysis**'. I will put down all the facts known to us now." She started drawing a mind map on a sheet of paper.

1. Mother picked up the infection somewhere but did not transmit it to the three of us.

2. Her infection was not from anyone of us, as all the three of us tested negative today.

3. Would it be possible that one of us was positive yesterday but turned negative today? Unlikely. Covid2121 infection stays in the body for a minimum of ten days as per accepted opinion about Covid2121. Could be possible that the ten days got over only yesterday and hence we are negative today. Possible

4. Mother got infected in Chennai only as Covid2121 infection shows up in three days. They could not have picked up the infection at Madurai.

5. They were quarantined in a separate room in the house. They never went out anywhere.

6. Both of us too did not go anywhere out of the house after we returned from Madurai. The infection happened in the last three days which means there is no possibility of one of us picking up the infection from outside.

7. No guest visited us in the last three days. We did not go to any shop.

8. Vipul and Vinitha then listed the people who visited the house since Wednesday, the day Vinitha's parents reached Chennai

   a) One grocery delivery and one vegetable / fruit delivery and Vipul confirmed that both deliveries were done by robots.

   b) Medicine ordered by Varad got delivered on Friday through a human.

   c) Servant maid came on Thursday but was asked not to come afterwards.

   d) Gene correction medicine was delivered to them but that was also a robot delivery.

9. We tested every individual in this house and all showed negative.

"Where are we now in our Root Cause?" Vinitha looked up at Vipul.

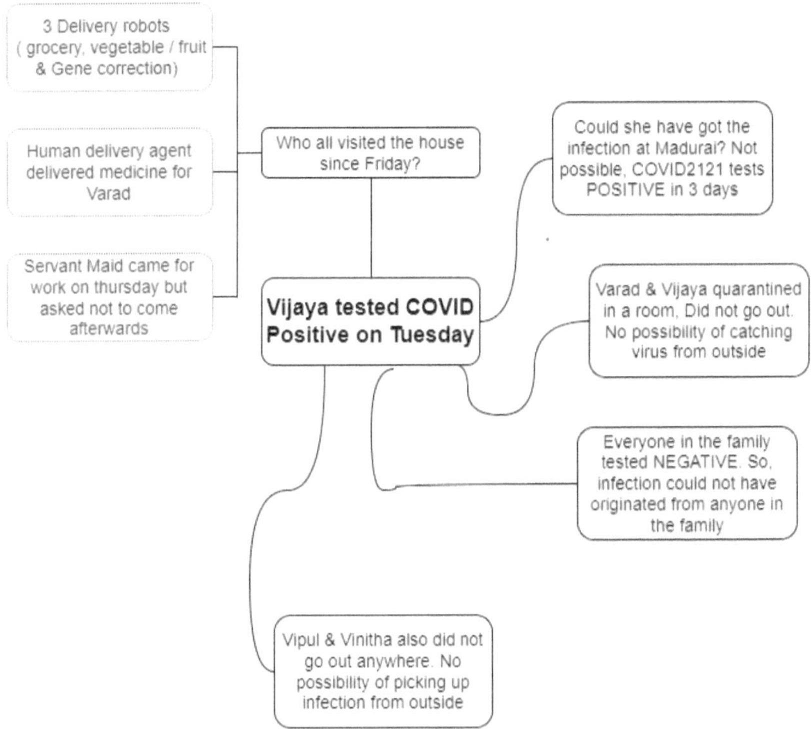

"You have come to the end of the paper and have no more space to draw in this paper. You must either use the backside or I must go and get you another sheet. That is all I could infer." Vipul laughed.

Vinitha did not appreciate the joke and gave a scornful look. "I have some inferences."

"We must just check one delivery agent and our servant maid to rule out the possibility that the virus could have come from any outsider. Help me to trace this medicine delivery boy. I will take care of our servant maid." Vinitha said

"How does it matter if it has come from any one of them? Nobody bothers to trace the Root Cause like this. It is very difficult." Vipul was not convinced.

"No, I want to trace. I have always been trained to get to the Root Cause and I have a strange feeling that we are getting at something very interesting."

Vipul got the contact details of the delivery boy in the next hour and ordered an RTPCR test on him. The result came as negative two hours after the test. Vinitha took an RTPCR test on the servant maid and that also turned out to be negative.

"There were only five humans from whom amma could have caught the infection and all five of them have tested negative today, which means none of them got infected in the last ten days."

"You said the gestation period could be three days. Is it possible that any one of these is in the infection gestation period and thus shows negative? Is it possible to infect another individual during the gestation period?" Vipul considered all the possibilities.

"Good thinking. I don't know. Let me check with the experts." Vinitha called a number and spoke for some time.

"My friend who is a doctor says it is highly impossible. Anyway, we can test all these five once again tomorrow. Let us rule out all possibilities." Vinitha was always very systematic.

"You said amma was in touch with only nine and five tested negative. Can it mean that it is possible to have come from the other four?" Vinitha asked.

"Not possible, because the other four were robots. Not heard of robots getting virus infection." Vipul replied

"Hold on. You mentioned, 'Not heard of…" **You have not heard,** or **it is not possible at all. Root Cause Analysis** cannot be concluded based on hearsay." Vinitha put back the question.

"Good question and I don't have a ready answer. It is a general belief that microbial viruses cannot affect robots. Only cyber viruses do."

"We cannot go by perceptions. We must eliminate all the possibilities." Vinitha added.

"To eliminate, we must test Sevugan. We did not test everyone in this house. We left out Sevugan." Vipul said.

"That is because Sevugan is a robot." Vinitha replied but started thinking about it.

"I treat him as a friend, not as a robot, and he plays carrom with me. He can discuss Bhagavad Gita with me." Vipul somehow wanted to cheer up the mood.

"**Sevugan is your friend.**" Vinitha did not respond further for the next two minutes. "Sevu is your friend, so do you want a Covid2121 test to be done for your friend?" Vinitha repeated the same sentence multiple times to herself. With each time, she became more pensive.

Vipul could not understand why she was repeating the same message. He could only infer that something was going on in her mind. She was always a strange combination of logic and imagination. That was what attracted him to her from the beginning. He decided to give her some time.

"Covid2121 test for Sevugan. There is no option to test a robot. How will you test a robot? You cannot put a probe into his nose. The probe will break." Vipul laughed.

When they were discussing the possibilities and complexities of subjecting a robot to Covid2121 test, *Abra* switched on the wallboard and a priority channel announcement started.

"It is five days now since the strict lockdown was enforced but Covid2121 is not abating. The R-curve is getting steeper and steeper. R value is 1.8 now. The Government of India has taken all necessary steps to ensure strict lockdown but the spread is not slowing down. The daily infection has gone up to more than five lakhs yesterday, the steepest increase ever since the virus was reported. Scientists believe that the logarithmic curve will climb further. Scientists are puzzled as to how the virus is spreading so fast even during strict lockdown. There were protests about continuing the lockdown especially since the lockdown did not seem to be making any dent in the infection. The Government of India constituted a high-power committee consisting of five top virologists and top bureaucrats in India under the leadership of the health minister. The committee is in the process of reviewing the situation and has been mandated to submit its report to the Prime Minister within two days. New infection rate could be slowed down only if the scientists are able to find the cause for the rapid spread."

"Why is it still spreading **in spite of** strict lockdown?" Vipul asked.

"Spreading **because** of strict lockdown, possible." Vinitha smiled.

"I cannot understand. How could the lockdown increase the spread? Every country enforced lockdown. Why would they enforce a lockdown if that is increasing the spread? Does not sound logical."

"Not logical if you look at it through a normal eye".

"But look at it like this. The last lockdown was effective. How could it be not this time?"

She was on a roll. "Yes. So?" Vipul was waiting for the next question.

"What is the difference between the last lockdown and this one?" Vinitha quizzed.

"Better implementation? Stricter rules?"

"OK. But how?" The game continued.

"Better monitoring? More use of robots?"

"Good. You are coming to the point. The virus is different. It is more predictable. It has a clear three-day gestation period, five-day symptomatic and a total of 10 days infection. Very clear. Symptoms are more or less uniform."

So? Vipul was beginning to see some patterns. Vinitha began making it clearer. "The virus is different. The pattern is clear. There is almost no human contact. Still the virus spreads. The only differentiator is in the implementation. That is where we begin."

"But how?" Vipul was still not completely clear.

"For that, you must wait. I have some additional special information and I am looking at it from that perspective."

"Like what?"

"We have a doubt that Sevugan, better to say one of the robots, could be a reason for giving Covid to my mother."

"Doubt. Not yet confirmed."

"OK. Unverified but still a doubt. That is not the point here. Robots are the only differentiators in this lockdown. If robots are the reason for the spread, possibility of making contact with a robot and getting the virus increases during this kind of strict lockdown. We are in touch with our robot all the time."

"I agree. '*Critical Thinking*[5].'"

---

[5] Critical thinking - Critical thinking is the analysis of available facts, evidence, observations, and arguments to form a judgement.

"Power of unconventional thinking. I am trained in critical thinking."

"Alright. But robots don't get infected let alone transfer."

"That is where we are stuck. We need to find the gap."

"But I believe it will take some time for the spread to peak before it can start coming down. This is what happened during Wave 1 of Covid19. India had a lockdown then as well, but the virus was spreading during the lockdown and then the Prime Minister had to extend the lockdown four to five times before the virus spread started coming down. Why are they making such a big fuss now within six days?" Vipul asked.

"Because there are 100 years in between the two Covid viruses and the lockdown now is even stricter. There were minimal control mechanisms to enforce strict lockdowns in 2020. Work from home is very common now even when there is no lockdown whereas it was not so in the earlier instance. You don't need to travel even for medical emergencies except for deep surgical procedures. All companies switch to 100% work from home very quickly and easily nowadays. AI Robotics technology has improved significantly in the last 100 years, so much so that 20% of the workforce are robots now and robots can work in offices even during lockdowns. Tough field jobs are now given to robots. Even factories can be managed remotely using a few robots at the factory. That is the advantage of the technological revolution. With all these, lockdowns are enforced very strictly nowadays.

So, the expectation is that the spread rate should have come down within three days of the lockdown." Vinitha explained.

"Another reason is that the infection rates this time are much steeper than Covid19. Much as technology has improved in the last 100 years, the virus must also have improved in the last 100 years." Vipul laughed.

"They cannot find the cause for the spread and the infection rate is not going to come down on its own. I don't know why the government is depending only on virologists in the committee. This committee will not be able to achieve much. Take it from me." Vinitha said.

"Who else would you think are required on the committee? Only virologists have knowledge about Covid virus. Who else would have the knowledge on Covid?" Vipul replied.

"Not necessary. That is the closed mindset. That will not work out. I have a strange feeling that we are asking the virologists to solve a problem that has more to it than virology." Vinitha was firm.

"Who else would need to be included? Are you thinking you should be invited as a member?" Vipul teased.

"Yes. I should have been included." Vinitha was serious and did not like Vipul teasing her.

Vipul did not understand her reply though Vinitha said it firmly.

"Vinu. I agree and appreciate that you have read enough about Covid2121 on the Internet for the last three days. You talk very well about Covid2121. But that does not mean you are an expert in Covid2121 containment, and you should be included in the high-power committee. That is *far-fetched* even for the 'country's best ethical hacker'. Dreaming is good but don't dream about illogical opportunities." Vipul gave a long explanation.

Vinitha silently stared at him. In the normal course, she would have fired him for always underestimating her or undermining her. She was only staring silently at him. Vipul wondered if she even heard what he said. And perhaps relieved that she may not have.

"Why do you think your input would help to solve the Covid2121 issue? You are not a health care expert." Vipul lowered his voice as a sign of apology but persisted. Vinitha continued to be in a pensive mode and silent.

"Because I am the best cyber security expert in India." Vinitha stood up. She obviously did not like Vipul's long lecture.

Vipul still could not understand, "What would a cyber security expert do to solve a virus problem and that too a biological virus, not a cyber virus?"

"Nowadays cyber security experts can solve all kinds of problems. I cannot explain it to you now. You would think I am hypothesizing whereas I am not. Not making wild guesses either."

Vinitha's phone made a ting sound. It was an email of Sevugan's logs. She programmed the logs to be sent to her every 8 hours.

"Oh, God. I totally forgot this in the melee. I have one more very strong fact to support that I am not making wild guesses. Sevugan has been attacked. He seems to be running a compromised code now. I was to analyse the logs and the sniffer but forgot it totally. Let me get back to that work."

"What do you mean? Is Sevugan going to run roughshod?"

"I cannot guess that, but he has been attacked."

"Are you saying that the fact that Sevugan has been attacked has anything to do with him spreading Covid2121 to your mother?"

"Maybe."

"Why are you connecting two seemingly unconnected events?"

"I am wired to connect the unconnected. I don't have proof that both are connected. I am confident about both individually and it is highly unlikely that they are not connected." The statement seemed like a riddle to Vipul.

"Give me five minutes, I have some important work. I will come back." Vipul left urgently. It was unlike Vipul, and Vinitha sensed something different about Vipul.

Just when Vinitha got up to leave the room, her phone started ringing and it was a call from her close friend, Vani. Vani informed Vinitha that she tested positive for Covid and was taken to a hospital forcefully by the corporation authorities though she did not want to go to the hospital. She had a one-year-old daughter, and she was checking with Vinitha if she could be of any help as her husband was finding it difficult to manage the baby. They had no other relatives in Chennai.

Before answering her request, Vinitha asked her the question, "Where did you get your infection from?"

Vani was a very good friend but she could not understand and appreciate the brusqueness in Vinitha's tone.

"I don't know. I did not try to find out. Could be from anybody. Anyway, does not matter now." Vani replied.

"No. It matters a lot. Don't leave it like that. If you don't find the root cause, your husband could get infected and possibly your baby also. Who will take care of the baby if your husband gets infected?"

"Oh my God. Don't scare me further. I cannot imagine what will happen to my daughter if my husband also gets infected. But he is taking a lot of precautions. He is confident that he will not get infected. He is religiously following everything prescribed by the government."

"That is not a guarantee. My mother followed all possible precautions, but she got infected. Be careful. The only way to stop it would be to investigate the source of your infection."

"How would I know? Very difficult."

"OK. I will ask you one question. Do you have a house robot?"

"Of course, we are staying alone in Chennai with a one-year-old baby. I started working after my maternity leave. We cannot manage without a house robot. We have a robot."

"Yes. I saw the robot last time when I visited you at your house and it is an NGN robot. Either switch off the robot or dump it in the Bay of Bengal if you want to be sure that your husband should not get Covid2121."

Vani wondered if Vinitha had gone mad because her mother got infected with Covid2121 but simply said, "Thanks for your advice," and disconnected the call.

Vinitha did not bother and rushed to her office room. Vipul came back from his errand and asked her, "What happened?" But she was not interested in replying.

Vipul ran behind her, "You behaved funny with Vani. Poor soul."

"I understand but I could not hide my enthusiasm. I will seek an apology from her later. Forget about it. Do you know what robot Vani is using?"

"Yes, I remember her robot greeted us with filter coffee when we visited her last month to see her kid. It must be a NGN robot."

"Do you know if it is from Robogenius?"

"I would not know that. I did not check the brand name."

"OK. I will get that information. No worries."

"What are you trying to hint at?"

"Look at this, said Vinitha in her excited voice.

1. I have this nagging doubt that my robot transmitted Covid to my mother.

2. There is an unanswered question as to how a patch released to cure a vulnerability turn buggy. Never heard of it before but it happened just before Covid2121 spread. This cannot be a coincidence.

3. Now Sevugan has been attacked. Something is seriously amiss with the robots, especially NGN robots from Robogenius.

4. Two robots showed wrong behaviour as soon they were upgraded to v7.4.1 which is not a 'Denial of Service' behaviour"

"*one swallow doesn't make a summer*. This is an old proverb. One Sevugan attacked and one mother infected does not explain six million infections. They could be unrelated incidents." Vipul replied.

"My job is to connect the dots and I do that very well. I have a strange feeling that I have a clear line between these dots. I will find out which dots it connect very soon."

"I don't think so. The dots are on two different pages."

"I will make you agree that the dots are on the same page and that too in a straight line."

"How will you do that?"

"Wait. I have an idea but will not tell you now. You will understand after I find out the answers."

Vinitha had an office room at home as she had to work often outside office hours on important assignments with complete secrecy and privacy. Vinitha's office room was not accessible even for Vipul. Vinitha went inside her office room and locked herself. Vipul knocked on the door a few times and then gave up.

WEDNESDAY 23ᴿᴰ APRIL 2121

bra continued to greet Vipul with the same Covid2121 alert message every morning. He got irritated and said, "*Abra*, abort the good morning routine".

He thought, "Why cannot the government change the message if they don't want to remove the message. Getting bored with the same message". He thought of disabling the 'good morning alarm' message. He could not disable the prefix message, but he should have the option to disable the good morning routine.

He sneaked into Vinitha's office room before going to the kitchen for his coffee. The door was open. Vinitha was curled up in her chair and was sleeping. She was all tousled and looked so vulnerable. She might have gotten up in between and slept again. He was both proud of her and worried about her. If only she knew how worried he was, she would perhaps be furious. 'Do you think I am a kid?' kind of anger.

But he could not help it. Vipul went inside the room and woke her up. She woke up with a startle, "Where am I?"

Vipul hugged her and said, "You mentioned some hunch about the uncontrollable spread of Covid2121 and you were searching for more data the whole night. What is your hunch?"

Vinitha did not want to share hunches even with Vipul. She was looking for some concrete information to validate her hunch. She was hopeful that Vipul might probably share some insights. "Vipul, the only information I now have is that there are two confirmed infections from our close circle and in both the cases a robot, an NGN robot, was the source of Covid2121 infection. I could not get any leads beyond this."

"I also thought about it. But that is not substantial information to arrive at any clue. It could be a piece of incidental information with no connection to the final answer. You don't have statistically enough data."

"We cannot leave it like that. Any small clue will open the door. For us now, Sevugan is the key to the chest where the answers to our puzzle lie."

"How do we prove it?"

"I am going to do whatever you said yesterday. Let us do a Covid test for Sevugan."

"I never asked for a Covid test for Sevugan. I don't know if it is even possible."

"You said we tested everyone in the house except Sevugan."

"That was a joke. I never thought you would take it seriously. If we ask anyone to do a Covid test for Sevugan, they will laugh at us. I don't know if it is required or even possible. I think you are going behind a piece of inconsequential and incidental information that your mother was not in touch with anyone else other than the three of us and Sevugan. It might be possible that she interacted with some neighbour but forgot to mention it to you."

"My first lesson on problem solving from my mentor, my first boss, is never to ignore any fact as inconsequential. He used to say - **No information is inconsequential, and nothing is impossible to analyse – these are the two most important axioms in problem solving.**"

"So, you are saying it is possible to do an RTPCR test on Sevugan based on whatever your mentor said."

"Yes, nothing is impossible."

"Then ask your mentor to come and do an RTPCR test for Sevugan." Vipul was getting irritated.

"OK. I will try but not sure though."

Vinitha and Vipul called various testing centres to ask for a Covid2121 test for Sevugan. But everyone laughed at them when they asked for a Covid test for a robot. They could hear one of them commenting loudly, "The government released a whole list of aftereffects of Covid2121 infection, but I now know one more. This is madness. These people might have gotten Covid2121 infection. I must report this new finding to the government."

Vinitha understood but did not bother. She never bothered about comments when she was on a mission. She simply ignored it.

"Covid2121 test for a robot? We cannot run any medical tests on robots. It is unrobotic to run medical tests on a robot. You can run hardware and software diagnostics on robots but not medical tests. If you want, I can suggest you a good agency to run full diagnostics on your robot. Do you want?" One testing center asked.

Vinitha got furious and banged the phone, "I don't need to run any diagnostic other than the Covid2121 test."

"Recessive mindset. Nobody is willing to test Sevugan. What to do?" Vinitha was furious.

"Be calm. You need to explain your theory to them. If you just ask for a test on a robot, nobody will do it."

Vinitha used her influence and one of her contact managed to get an agency to send a person to test Sevugan. One laboratory technician with Covid protective suit and a test kit in hand knocked at their door in 45 minutes.

"I have been asked to do a Covid test in this house. Whom should I test?"

Vinitha called Sevugan and pointed at him.

"On a robot?" He referred to his handbook of procedures on Covid tests from his mobile phone but could not find any clue on how to do an RTPCR test for a robot.

Vinitha said, "I already told your centre head that it is a test on a robot. He agreed. Has he not briefed you?"

"No. He just mentioned doing an RTPCR test and it is asymptomatic. I am wondering where I can insert my swab. We are instructed to collect from the nose and tongue. Robots don't have a tongue and their nose is completely empty inside except for smell sensory organs. What is the point in collecting a sample from the nose or the tongue?"

"Why don't you collect the sample from the palm? I read that the hands and palms of next generation robots are made of a material called polyserex and they are close to human skin in terms of sensory perception. Polyserex can sense a prick, fire, cut, etc. Sevugan is a next generation robot." Vipul suggested.

The technician was not convinced. "I agree that the palm is the best part to collect samples if at all I need to collect but I feel it is not required."

Vinitha said, "Never mind. We are paying anyway. Just collect from his palms and send it for testing."

The technician took out two swabs and rolled the swabs on both the hands of Sevugan around the entire palm. He then finally asked Sevugan to hold the swab tightly in his clenched palm.

Sevugan opened his palm, everyone looked at his open palm only to realize that the swab was broken. The technician got irritated and asked Sevugan not to hold it so tight.

Sevugan shot back, "you told me to hold the swab tight and I did exactly the same. You should give clear instructions; you humans are like that. You give some instruction and then you blame us for following the instruction religiously."

The technician took another swab and placed it on Sevugan's palm. This time he asked him to just roll it lightly on the palm.

Sevugan asked, "Why is this man rolling some funny tubes on my hands? Can I know?"

Vinitha replied, "We are testing you for Covid2121 because amma got the infection, just to be sure."

"You should have told me before subjecting me to the test. We robots cannot be subjected to any biological test. This is in clause 14a (ii) of the Robot Control Act. Do you know what the punishment is for violating the clause?"

"This is a special case Sevugan and we have already taken the necessary permission. We have not done any biological tests on you. We only collected samples from your palm. That is not a biological test." Vipul patted Sevugan's shoulder.

"Your reply is not convincing. You should have still told me in advance. I am not a bonded labourer here. Anyway, if you are suspecting me to be infected by the Covid virus, you should have quarantined me. Why are you still asking me to do your chores?

You quarantine humans when you suspect them of Covid infection, and they enjoy a holiday during quarantine." Sevugan thought he had outsmarted Vipul.

"One minute. Where did you come across bonded labourer? The practice of Bonded Labour was abolished 100 years back. No one living now would know the meaning of bonded labour." Vipul said.

"I told you that I got interested in Tamil literature. I now started reading the Tamil stories written by author Sujatha from the Internet archives. There was a reference about கொத்தடிமை (bonded labour) in one of his books and I looked at the meaning in the dictionary." Luckily Sevugan forgot about his protest against Covid2121 test on him.

"Oh, I understand now." Vipul said.

"Do you know that the author Sujatha wrote about a robot like me in his story as early as the 1990s? He wrote about an intelligent robot dog called Juno." Sevugan was very excited narrating about intelligent robots. "Sujatha is a genius." Sevugan added.

"OK. OK. Sujatha is not waiting for your certification." Vipul commented grumpily.

"You are jealous that you have still not read any story of Sujatha whereas I already completed 15 stories." Sevugan retorted and went into the kitchen.

xx

Sevugan's test report came on Vipul's phone in two hours. It was Covid negative.

"Sevugan's test report is negative. Do you now agree that robots cannot be the source of infection for humans?" Vipul asked.

"Not necessarily. The only confirmed conclusion is that we can hug Sevugan right now and we would not get infected. We cannot infer anything more than that. I am back to square one." "Moreover, we are still not sure if rolling the swab on the palm is the right procedure to test the presence of virus in skin. The guy who collected sample was clueless" Vinitha added.

Sevugan came to the hall on hearing his name and asked, "What is the status of my RTPCR test? You have an obligation to inform me about the status."

"Negative," said Vipul. Vinitha did not want to look up at Sevugan.

"I read about Covid2121 and RTPCR report after my sample was collected. It was unnecessary. The virus can infect only a biological body. We robots don't have cells which can get infected."

"Thanks for your lesson. I have read enough about Covid2121." Vinitha mumbled indicating that she did not need lessons from a robot.

"I did not hear you say the magic word 'sorry'. I am programmed to say sorry to you even when it does not fit in the list of reasons you have to say sorry for. It is your ego" Sevugan left the hall.

Vinitha looked at Vipul with an eye language that Vipul correctly understood to mean that his configuration fine-tuning had not helped.

Vipul came near Vinitha and said in a low voice, "I reduced his 'learning index' and he is not aware of that. It will take some time to take effect. Anyway, what he has asked is also fair. We should have informed him of his test result and could have told him sorry. A simple sorry would have solved the stalemate."

"You and your robot. You go and fall at his feet. I am not going to say sorry. You love your robot more than your wife." Vinitha mumbled and stood up to leave.

"Put this thought of robots getting infected with Covid to **rest** and take some **rest**. We anyway don't have to go to the office today." Vipul said.

"One correction. I never said robots can get infected and I am still saying robots could possibly be aiding in spreading the infection. There is a **huge difference between the two**. I will not change my opinion because of Sevugan's negative test report."

Just then, *Abra* played a giggling noise and the wall screen came on. The duo understood that the news ahead was funny.

"Covid2121 is spreading unabated. Global leaders are shocked and clueless as to how the virus is spreading so fast despite lockdowns in almost all countries. 72 countries around the world have enforced lockdown and travel restrictions between countries as well as within the countries. Roads and airways are empty."

Video images of empty roads, empty shopping malls and empty airways played.

Dr. Vittal Lobo came on the screen and announced, "We were first focusing on the impact of Covid2121 virus and the treatment for it. We have greater clarity now on the possible impacts and the treatment methods. We managed to reduce the number of deaths significantly. The mortality rate due to Covid2121 is coming down and will come down significantly in the days to come. Our next focus is on reducing the spread. We do not have any clue yet on how the virus is spreading so fast though we minimized all possible human-human contacts. We have very limited human-human interaction now except among family members and the virus is still spreading. We have no answer yet on this. We have suggested to the government to enforce separation within families as the next step to contain the virus spread. It is lockdown outside the home and separation within the home. That is our recommendation."

"Crazy. What is he talking about? How can we have separation? He has gone crazy. He is suggesting we suffer because of the failure of the scientists to find out correct answers." Vinitha shouted.

"Don't shout. There is logic in what he says. How to control the spread otherwise? The lockdown is not helping. People are locked in within their homes and the virus is still spreading. The only way left is to bring lockdown within the families."

Abra woke up again and flashed a Red Alert briefing.

The Central Minister of Health came on the screen with a *namaste* and started talking about the imposition of the new rule of separation within the house.

"We are enforcing a new restriction called 'Separation within house' from today. This will be in addition to the lockdown. Our new Covid mantra is **LOCKDOWN OUTSIDE HOME & SEPARATION INSIDE HOME.**"

"Separation inside home means you will strictly avoid any human-to-human contact within the home as well. Each family member needs to be constrained within their identified room. Couples will need to move to separate rooms. Avoid sharing anything including clothes, food and toiletries between the family members. Detailed instructions about separation within house will be available in your Inbox within ten minutes. Thanks for your cooperation. Those who do not have enough isolation space within the home will be accommodated in special Covid quarantine centres built by the government. The government has built enough temporary shelters for Covid2121."

"Lockdown & Separation will bring down Covid2121."

"To safeguard the interests of our dear citizens, we formed a flying squad of Health Inspectors and the inspector could make a surprise visit to any house to inspect and verify if all the houses are following separation guidelines and anyone found to be not following could be penalized. Jai Hind."

"Crazy. They are going crazy. Separation is not going to help. They are working on a single-minded focus that the virus is spread by humans. Lack of critical thinking. He is talking about penalizing people for not following separation guidelines. What for?" Vinitha shouted at the top of her voice.

"I have a big problem. If all family members are constrained within their rooms, who will cook? Does he mean, everyone must set up a mini kitchen within their room?" Vipul had a genuine doubt.

"You and your government. Go and refer to your separation instructions from the news brief. Check and tell me if Sevugan can cook and supply each one separately. Sevugan would have additional work and I am not sure if he would take up additional work without protest." Vinitha cribbed.

"Unfortunately, I am not able to proceed further in my thought process. I am still looking for that one clue that will break all the barriers. I am not getting there. It is just there. I can feel it. Just a small piece of this large puzzle is missing."

THURSDAY, 24ᵀᴴ APRIL 2121

The next day started with another interesting problem.

The doorbell rang and Vipul saw in his video door phone the next-door neighbour, Narayan. Narayan was his walking friend. Since walking on the roads was banned, Vipul had not met or spoken to Narayan for the past six days. Narayan as well as his wife Veda were good friends of Vipul & Vinitha. They had unrestricted access to the house and kept popping in and out quite often. But the situation was different that day. Vipul was not interested to let him in with so much melee happening in the family. Vinitha had given very strict instructions not to let anyone into the house and Vipul was worried about another big argument if he let Narayan in. Vipul spoke to Narayan through the video door phone and asked him the reason. He apologized to him for not letting him in.

Narayan wanted to consult Vipul on a problem with his house robot. Everyone in the colony knew Vipul's interest in robotics and considered him an expert in robotics. Vipul suggested a video call instead. Narayan sounded offended by the unfriendly act, but Vipul would not budge. Narayan went back to his house and called Vipul over the video phone. Narayan narrated a peculiar problem and asked for Vipul's advice.

Naryan's house robot had become very old and was largely ineffective. The robot's vision had almost failed, and hearing was largely impaired. There were some mechanical problems as well and the robot was not able to move normally. Since the robot was of a very old version, he was finding it difficult to rectify the problems. Narayan was feeling bad to discard the robot as it had served him well for a long time.

Narayan asked, "Is it legally allowed to switch off a robot when the robot is still in service?"

Vipul replied, "There is a provision in the Robot Control Act under the clause 'mercy killing of robots' on how to stop a functioning robot. It is permitted under certain conditions. Approval needs to be taken from the Registrar of Robots. They will inspect the condition of the robot and give consent if the robot can be stopped. You will get approval only if the robot is in a totally unusable condition. Once the approval is received, you need to surrender the robot (only) to an authorized robot recycler and submit the proof to the Registrar of Robots."

Vipul further asked, "Whom did you consult for servicing your robot?"

"Robocure Global, a well-known robot service company." Narayan replied.

"I know them. They are good but they are generalists. They can cure general problems only. Don't go to generalist robot service companies for such advanced problems. There are specialists to attend to specific problems. If the problem is with the eyesight and hearing, I can suggest a good 'sensory specialist robot doctor' who can do complex operations to restore the eyesight and hearing in a robot. Similarly, I know a mechatronics specialist who can solve problems of all kinds of mechanical joints in robots. You should first take him to specialists before taking a decision on mercy killing." Vipul suggested.

"Is it worth Vipul? He is already ten years old. Will he keep giving issues again and again?"

"There is no age limit for robots, unlike humans. If the specialists can treat your robot properly, he can become quite normal and resume normal service. That is the advantage with the robots. The specialists I will suggest are good. They have cured more complex problems and the robots are giving good service after the cure." Vipul suggested. "I know it is very painful to lose the services of a faithful robot. Try checking with the specialists and then take a decision to decommission only if the specialists are not able to resurrect him."

"But my robot is not a next generation robot like Sevugan. Is it advisable to swap him for a next generation robot? Is it possible to upgrade him to next generation?"

"First point, it is not possible to upgrade previous generation robots to next generation robots as the design of NGN has been completely changed. For the second question, I would suggest not abandoning a working robot in favour of an NGN robot. You get lots of cool features in NGN, no doubt about it. But remember, you will lose the intelligence of your robot that has been acquired over the last ten years. He would have got used to your family, your family's requirements, etc. It will take time for a new robot, even if it is an NGN robot, to get that learning and adaptation. Vinitha is still not getting used to Sevugan, even after ten months."

"True. He is very affectionate to my son and daughter. My family also likes him a lot. I would prefer not losing him."

"Yes. The knowledge gathered in a robot is more important than a few cool new features and it is not possible to transfer the knowledge from the old generation robots to new generation robots. I would recommend you first to explore all options to cure your robot and it is possible."

"Sounds good. That is why I came to you. I am clear now. Please send the contacts of the sensory specialist and mechatronics specialist. I will check with them." Narayan was happy.

"They will charge a bomb though. Be ready. They are specialists, after all. They will prescribe lots of diagnostic tests and you might end up changing lots of expensive parts. We cannot help it if we need the services of an expert specialist." Vipul added.

Just when he disconnected the call, Vipul heard dry coughs from the living room and got worried. Hearing a cough was like hearing the sounds of bombs then. Vipul rushed to the living room.

He found Vinitha sitting next to her father and taking thermometer reading.

The thermometer said, "Temperature is 99.5°F with 99.5% accuracy. This is 0.9°F above the normal temperature. This increase could be temporary and due to multiple factors. However, considering the Covid2121 threat, recommend taking a Covid RTPCR test asap."

"We were very careful, and I don't know how you got infected." Unlike the earlier instance, Vinitha sounded sure that the increase in temperature was due to Covid2121 infection this time.

"Yes, I did not let in my good friend Narayan but sent him back. He was upset." Vipul made it a point to mention his sacrifice to Vinitha.

"You and your stupid friend. Does it matter now?" Vinitha was upset which came out as irritation.

Vinitha immediately ordered another RTPCR test for the three of them. She thought for a second and said, "Include my robot also, you did a test on him yesterday."

Vijaya was still in the hospital and was recovering well as per the latest update received from her phone. Vinitha was more worried about her father than her mother as her father was a heart patient. She immediately dialled and updated his physician.

"We could have remained in Madurai. We would have been spared." Varad said.

"Why do you say so, uncle? Why do you think your infection is because of this house? Covid is spreading fast, and the prediction is that every citizen of India will get infected in another forty days. All of us will get infected unless they identify the source of this infection quickly." Vipul tried to console him.

"No. I think there is some bad omen in this house. Otherwise, why would both of us get infected within two days?"

"You have still not been tested. Why do you jump to conclusions?" Vipul interrupted.

"I am sure I have the infection."

"How are you sure?"

"Your amma got confirmed for the infection from the same house and I now have the symptoms. I am sure. There is something wrong with this place." He repeated.

Vipul remembered to inform and convince Sevugan before the test technician came for collecting the samples.

Sevugan asked, "I tested negative yesterday and why one more test today?"

Vipul replied, "appa was also negative yesterday, but we are testing him again today."

"He is coughing. That is why you are testing him. I am not coughing. I will never cough. We robots never get cold, cough, sneeze, belch, etc., like you humans. Why should you test me again today?"

"I am not coughing. I don't have a fever. I tested negative. I am going to test again today. It is just for your own safety. That is it." Vipul said.

"I don't believe. These tests are not for my safety. Madam is suspecting that I passed the infection to amma and appa and that is why you are subjecting me to repeat the tests. Madam's theory is wrong. Robots cannot get virus infections. It is not in our design."

Vinitha was happy that Sevugan referred to her as madam. "I agree with your theory, Sevugan. But let us still complete this test. You see, all of us in the family are getting tested. You are also part of the family. Hence you are also getting tested". This seemed to impress Sevugan, at least silence him.

Just then the test technician came and took the samples from all four of them. He remembered to tell Sevugan to be gentle when placing the swab on his palm.

The test results came over the phone in the next two hours. As expected, Varad tested positive and the other three of them tested negative.

Vinitha requested her father to be admitted in the same room as that of her mother so that both could give company to each other.

While waiting for the ambulance to come, Vinitha asked, "How did appa test negative yesterday but positive today?"

"Simple, because he got the infection two days after amma's infection." Vipul replied.

"I know that. I am trying to deduce the logic. This means he contacted the source two days later than amma, as per confirmed Covid2121 behaviour." Vinitha again went into deep thinking.

"There is one more logical deduction. It is the same source that infected amma as there is no other source of infection possible. The source of infection must be in this house only." Vinitha started filling up new bubbles in the mind maps in her notepad.

"Could it be possible that he picked up the virus on the same day but amma got infected faster and appa got infected two days later? That might be the case." Vipul suggested.

"I know for sure it is not possible. I read that Covid2121 shows predictable behaviour in terms of the time period required for the virus to show the symptoms and in the test report after getting the first contact. This is always the same two days in all the infected cases. This is contrary to the behaviour of Covid19. Anyway, let me not make wrong assumptions based on unverified information on the Internet. Let me call and find out from a good doctor." Vinitha dialled a number and chatted for the next five minutes.

"I called a doctor and got the clarification. Covid2121 behaviour shows that it takes the same time always, just two days to show the symptoms and for the infection to start. It is either infection or no infection. Delayed infection is not known from any of the tests done, even for one day. Infection can be symptomatic or asymptomatic, but the cycle remains the same. That is the pattern for Covid2121 and it is confirmed in all the Covid2121 cases."

"What do you deduce then?" Vipul could not understand.

"This means appa got in touch with the virus two days later than amma but in a similar fashion, probably from the same source. It is for sure that appa also got the infection from within this house and not from anyone outside this house."

"Could it be possible that if we had practiced separation as recommended by Dr. Lobo, we could have stopped appa's infection?" Vipul asked.

"Dump you and your separation theory into the Bay of Bengal." Vinitha was furious. Vipul knows that 'Bay of Bengal' means she is irritated.

"First part of your statement could be true but how are you sure that they got the infection in the same fashion?" Vipul would not get hurt by such statements. He was used to them. He also knew that Vinitha was normally cheerful, and these were brief flashes especially when she was on to something. He called it *Vinithitis*, to himself of course. And to her, when she was in a good mood.

"Because both remained at home only, and did not meet any third party, **there were two outsiders in the house last week but no outsider in the last three days**. Note down this very carefully. The delivery boy and the servant maid also tested negative and - hence they cannot be the source. We don't have any pet at home, the only people both got in touch with are Vipul, Vinitha and Sevugan." Vinitha gave her rationale.

"Yes. I did not allow my good friend Narayan also." Vipul smiled.

"Why are you parroting the same again and again? That happened today and there is a gestation period of two days for Covid2121 to show symptoms. It is irrelevant data in our investigation. The infection could not have come from Narayan even if he was allowed in today."

"So, you are saying that both of them got the infection from Vipul or Vinitha or Sevugan." Vipul started his 'think-ping-pong' with her. They did this very often. "But all three have tested negative."

"Yes. The difference is that we both can get infected but Sevugan cannot. So the infection is not from Vipul and Vinitha because they remain negative till this minute."

"If one of us were the source of infection, we would have been infected already. We remain uninfected still. So, are you deducing that the infection came from Sevugan?" Vipul asked in a low voice checking if Sevugan was anywhere nearby.

"But Sevugan is also negative like our test reports. We took two tests on him, and both were negative. **Sevugan's test report is not**

any different. How can you say that Sevugan was the source?" Vipul started scratching his head.

Vinitha suddenly jumped from the sofa and turned to Vipul, "What did you say just now?"

Vipul knew that her sudden enthusiasm must be because she got some spark. "Sevugan's test report is also negative, and our test reports are also negative and no difference."

"There is one big difference my dear sweet stupid husband. We are humans and Sevugan is a robot."

"That is known. Why would that matter here? You only said the robot was also to be tested and the robot could have caused the infection. You are now telling us that we are humans and Sevugan is a robot. You are contradicting."

"Think, You intelligent nut. We are humans and we are negative for two continuous days which clearly rules out us having the virus in the last ten days. Remember, the Covid2121 virus remains in the body for minimum ten days. If we have to be the virus carrier, we would have gotten infected and the infection would show in the tests for a minimum of ten days. I read everything about this virus."

"Sevugan is also not infected as he is still negative." Vipul repeated the same sentence.

"Yes, but the difference is that Sevugan is a robot and the virus cannot go inside his body. Do you know that the virus can remain on a surface for a short period, about one hour? Two negative tests rule out the possibility of us being the virus carriers as the virus would have gone inside our body and infected us but that is not the case with Sevugan. His negative test report confirms that he was not having the virus during the test and a maximum of one hour prior to the test, that too only in his palms, during the two tests." Vinitha explained.

Vipul thought about this for some time and suddenly spurted out "So you are saying that We cannot be virus carriers at all as we were tested negative, but Sevugan could still be a virus carrier as robots could be transient virus carriers"

"Yes, you summarized it very nicely. Now, combine this with other information you have, and a complete picture will emerge"

"Like what?"

"Other useful facts we know, we know that Sevugan has been attacked, we know that only two robots out of 8 running v7.4.1 had problem and the other six did not face any problem with the patch upgrade" "Soch lo…" Vinitha smiled exuberantly.

"Unconnected dots seem to be falling in line now. Yes, it is possible that the new version v7.4.1 created some issue with the robots who have already been compromised and Robogenius withdrew the new release because they were not comfortable with what they saw. You solved the last riddle" Vinitha kissed Vipul.

"Let us summarize. Sevugan gets the virus in his body, but the virus was not in his palm during the time we tested him. You are saying that he had the virus but did not get infected."

"Recollect what I already told you. I am not saying that Sevugan got infected. I am aware that he cannot get infected. All I am saying is that somehow Sevugan took the virus to appa and amma. We did not infect amma or appa which means Sevugan took the virus to them, for sure." Vinitha added.

"Plausible, theoretically. But I am still not confident in this theory. If we are not getting the virus, how could Sevugan alone get exposed to the virus?"

"Do you mean to say that Sevugan, and of course the other two robots as well, has been attacked and the after-effect of this attack is that they spread Covid2121 to humans in their contact?" Vipul was good at deducing logic. Which is why they do this intellectual ping-pong often.

"Possible. Not only that. Like these three robots, thousands of attacked robogenius robots could be spreading the virus. I forgot to check this. I need to check if Vani's robot was also compromised. Highly possible."

"But it still looks absurd to me. If Sevugan has to be the source of infection, what is the source of him getting the virus? He is also staying inside the house and he did not get in touch with anyone like us."

"I agree. That is still a big hole in my theory. I don't have any clue as to how he could have gotten in touch with that deadly virus. Let me do some interrogation with appa until the ambulance arrives." Vinitha went near her father.

"Did you meet or come within a ten-meter radius of anyone in the last 2-3 days?" Vinitha started her interrogation.

"None, other than you and *mapillai*. You stopped the servant maid as well. The servant maid came only for the first day we came here. I did not see her after that."

"What about your medicine delivery?"

"*Mapillai* took the delivery and made the payment. I did not go anywhere near the visitor. *Mapillai* gave the medicines to me."

"Who is giving your daily medicines?"

"I take it myself. Why do I need someone to give me the medicines?"

"Good. You told me and your *mapillai*. But you did not mention Sevugan."

"Of course, I as well as your amma interact with Sevugan on a daily basis but he is a robot and not a human."

"Leave that to me, we have not been careful, like many other people in this world, thinking that a robot cannot bring a virus. Tell me what are the things that are done in common between both you and amma and what you do differently."

"Both of us are nice gentle human beings." Varad did not lose his sense of humour even after coming to know that he was infected.

"Ayyo, appa. Be serious!"

"Umm, Sevugan brings me coffee every morning, but your mother does not take coffee in the morning. He serves food, all three times and both of us eat together. Could that be a possibility to get infected?"

"Possible. But all of us eat together ever since you came here. You remember, both of us did not go to the office after you came as the lockdown was announced the same day. If you got infected when taking food, we could also have gotten infected. So less likely but cannot be ruled out."

"That cannot be ruled out like that. It is possible that our immunity is good and hence we were not infected. We are still younger and healthy anyway." Vipul interrupted.

"I know you are a good programmer. Programmers possess strong logical skills. True. For a moment, let us assume that it is less likely. I am thinking anything else, you and amma do together but we were not part of it."

"Nothing much. We do not disturb Sevugan for anything else. Oh. I remember. We developed the habit of taking *panankalkandu* milk at night. Your amma started the habit and I followed her. We added *panankalkandu* to your grocery bill and requested Sevugan to give us *panankalkandu* milk every night."

"When did this practice start?"

"About six months ago."

"Ayyo, when did you start after coming to this house?"

"Let me recollect. We got the grocery delivery on Friday and started drinking *panankalkandu* milk from Friday night."

"Both of you started on Friday?"

"Let me recollect. I remember now. I did not take it on Friday & Saturday as I had digestive problems. I took it from Sunday onwards."

"This is very useful info appa. I am more convinced now."

PING…, sound came from Vinitha's phone. Vinitha looked at her phone and it was a chat message from Vanaja. The message read out in excited voice "Vinitha, I found very interesting information. Call me when you are free"

Vinitha quickly pressed CONNECT button. Vanaja "You could have called me"

"I know that your mother is Covid infected. I did not want to trouble you when you are not comfortable. That is why I sent the message"

"Vanaja, my father is also infected now"

"Oh God, please take care. We can discuss later"

"No. I am waiting for your interesting information. I am sure that would help me for my battle with Covid"

"I got response from one of our honeypots" Vanaja sounded excited.

"That is great. Which robot?"

"Not from a robot. None of the robot gave any information"

"Then"

"I loaded honeypot in many systems and one of the honeypot programmed to mimic a robogenius robot OS robatma sent me some information"

"That is a great idea to mimic robogenius. Normally done with honeypots. Which OS did you mimic?"

"I loaded honeypots for both v7.4.0 as well as v7.4.1"

"Which one responded?"

"With v7.4.0"

"As expected, What intelligence did you get?"

"It is an attempt to exploit 'Remote Code Execution' vulnerability"

"Any idea on the source?"

"That was very surprising. The source of attack was Robogenius master console system"

"Did you get any info about the exploit code?"

"Not able to, Vinitha. I need your help to decode. I downloaded the exploit code but not able to decipher the code. Since it is a mimicked system, I am not able to decipher the code. The exploit has something to do specific to the robogenius robot. The exploit is failing in the mimicked system but not able to find what is it trying to do. We may need the support of Robogenius to decipher the exploit code"

"Hold On. You mentioned that the attack source is the console software. Is not it?"

"Yes, Vinitha"

"Did you try honeypot in the console software?"

"I did not think about it. Sorry. I am getting your line of thought. You are suspecting that the console software could have got compromised already. Am I correct?"

"Yes. You got it"

"Sorry. Did not occur to me. Will try immediate and get back to you"

"Meanwhile, send me the code. I will try to research on that. I sent an escalation already through our CEO to Robogenius. I am expecting their response anytime now"

"This is very useful information Vanaja. Thanks a lot for your commitment. I am proud of you. Any other information?" Vinitha remembered not to be brusque.

"I was informed today that our Sales Head, Pankaj Mishra is down with Covid. He is in hospital. Nice man. I remember talking to him couple of days back and he was quite normal and full of zeal as usual. He answered my questions patiently though he is many levels senior to me. Our leaders should learn from him"

"What did you ask him. Anyway, nobody gets irritated with your questions. You developed nice way of questioning" Vinitha complimented.

"He is one of the two who reported problem with his robot when robogenius upgraded to v7.4.1. Do you remember that eight of our staff upgraded to v7.4.1 and only two out of the eight faced issue with the new version and Pankaj is one of the two who faced problem…." Vanaja went on.

"Hold on. Repeat again for me. Let me comprehend" Vinitha interrupted. Vanaja was aware that Vinitha got some new spark.

"We know that Sevugan is compromised and my mother and father are infected. Now you are telling me that Pankaj Mishra is infected and his robot had a problem with the new version and more specifically immediately after the new version was loaded. I feel both are connected"

"What are you hinting at?" Vanaja could not understand.

"Pankaj's robot is also compromised" Vinitha clarified. "Can we check with all those eight? If possible, right now" typical of Vinitha's style. She cannot resist when she is on a discovery.

Both called all the seven, other than Pankaj, and the discovery threw lot of light to their investigation. Apart from Pankaj, Kamala reported problem in her robot when upgrading to the new version and Kamala confirmed that her mother-in-law was hospitalized with Covid. Only one out of the six who did not face any issue with the version upgrade faced Covid infection in the family, other five were hale and healthy including everyone in their family. The five of them in fact got irritated when asked if any one of them in their family was infected with Covid virus.

"Let me guess your next move, Vinitha. Let me have the pleasure of guessing your line of thought" Vanaja was raring to go.

"Go Ahead"

"You want me to load the honeypot in the two robots which had the problem and check if they have also been compromised. You are feeling that both those robots have been compromised like Sevugan. Am I correct?"

"Bang On"

"Hold On. Why do you so say?" Vipul could not understand.

"You would understand if you had some experience with cyber security, but I am not going to explain to you now. Review this conversation once again and you will understand" Vinitha smiled mischievously.

"Ok. Vinitha. I have interesting work in hand. Let me get on with the work, honeypots" Vanaja was keen to get on with the work quickly.

"Hold on Vanaja. Why don't you load honeypots in all those 8 robots and check?" Vinitha added.

"You are being extraordinary, Vanaja. Thanks for the commitment" Vinitha was genuinely impressed.

"Thank you Vinitha. It is my pleasure to work for you"

The ambulance sounded the horn and Vinitha disconnected the call and packed all the essentials for Varad in a new overnight bag. Vipul remembered to add the *panankalkandu* bottle in the bag and said, "Uncle, I packed the *panankalkandu* in your bag. You can ask the nurse to give you *panankalkandu* milk every night. It would most likely be a robot nurse. Most of the nurses are robots nowadays."

"Forget about that stupid *panankalkandu*. You are being stupid Vipul. What is important? *Panankalkandu* is not important now." Vinitha said.

"Everything is stupid, and everyone is stupid for you." Vipul murmured, beginning to get irritated too.

After seeing off the ambulance, Vinitha came into the house.

Vipul remembered and asked her, "you said your friend Vani got infected yesterday and was worried about her child. Did you check what happened to them?"

Vinitha said, "I totally forgot. Thanks for reminding me."

"You behaved a little funny in the call yesterday." Vipul remembered and told her.

"I am sorry, I was not in my senses for the last two days. I was irritating you also." Vinitha threw in an apology. She called her friend Vani and spoke to her.

"As I feared, her husband is also infected and got admitted today. Poor girl. The baby is with their neighbour now. Pathetic scenario. Nobody should face this. How would a one-year-old baby survive without the care of the mother as well as the father? We should go and pick up the baby." Vinitha said.

"One more rationale aligned with your hunch. There is a house robot in her house as well. What a great similarity between you and your friend. Both use an NGN robot and two family members got infected in both families. It is the father and mother in your case and herself and her husband in the case of Vani. What a strange coincidence between two friends?" The ping pong appeared to continue. "I should probably check with some of our other friends who use an NGN robot at their house." Vipul added.

"Thanks a lot, Vipul. You spoke sensibly for the first time in the last week. I now know what needs to be done, thanks to Vani and her husband and my dear bright, smart, sweet, stupid husband. It is unfortunate that her suffering gave me useful clues." Vinitha rushed to her office room.

"What is this? I am stupid even when I give a very sensible idea." Vipul protested. But Vinitha was not to be seen there to listen to his protest.

Vipul went behind her calling knowing well that she must be on an interesting discovery, but Vinitha did not respond and locked herself up in her office room.

Vinitha accessed various reports on the list of Covid infections across the world. She could easily get access to the data as she had access due to government privilege. She was currently working on a Government of India project as an advisor and hence had privileged access to most of the sensitive data.

Vinitha sliced and diced the data across various dimensions — country, economic strata, gender, genetic background, the extent of lockdown implemented in each country / state, average life expectancy of each social group, literacy level, computer usage indicator, etc. She could get all the required information, courtesy of the high-power computer used by her and her high-speed backbone bandwidth. She projected various reports side by side for comparison and analysis. She could narrow down the following striking inferences after about half an hour of data analysis of Covid2121 data. She also searched for Covid19 data to compare the current pandemic dynamics with that of the earlier instance of the pandemic.

- Effectiveness of the lockdown did not correlate properly with the Covid2121 doubling rate. Very low correlation index, 0.23.

- There is a strong correlation on the development index of a territory with the Covid2121 doubling rate measured.

- Correlation is irregular with respect to vaccination. Existing Covid vaccinations indicate that the known vaccinations are not that effective against Covid2121.

- One striking piece of data that attracted her attention was, correlation is even stronger with the computer penetration level. Computer penetration level correlates strongly with the development index. The correlation of the doubling rate with the development index is 0.62 whereas the correlation of the doubling rate with the computer penetration index is 0.79.

She spent the next five minutes thinking deeply and suddenly picked up the reports and shouted, "Eureka, I got it. I got the clue. I'll get the answers."

She then took sample data from 100 Covid2121 patients tested on various dates since the pandemic. She took care to take the samples among the various criteria she had analysed before.. She called a higher official of National Citizens Registry known to her from one of her previous assignments. She requested an urgent report for the 100 Covid2121 positive reports on various parameters.

The report came to her Inbox in just four minutes. That is the power of data for the government. She loaded the report and zoomed in on each column. She took the zoom to the column "Type of house robot used" and a smile emerged from her lips. "Strange, the correlation between families with Covid infection and families with NGN robot is very high, 0.987!" She exclaimed.

She came out of her room and hugged Vipul and shouted, "I found out. I have the answer."

Vipul asked, "What is that answer?"

"What is unique with the next generation robots? My answer lies in that."

"Many things. Sevugan is a next generation robot." Vipul answered.

"I know that Sevugan is a next generation robot. That adds to my list of 100 samples. That is why I want to know about next generation robots. How are they different from the older robots?"

"In many ways, they come with more computing power to do deep learning algorithms. They learn faster. You cannot defeat a next generation robot in a game of chess. They learn very fast. Hmm. You know that. They come with more human-like features. You already experienced that as well. They can smell better than humans and they can feel touch. Their hearing power is five times that of humans. They are built with a material closely equivalent to that of human skin. A next generation robot can sense the pain of the cut, burn, etc." Vipul gave a lecture.

"I am not able to follow you now. Do me a favour, please. Download and send me all the features added in 'new generation robots'." Vinitha was about to leave.

"What has an NGN robot to do with Covid2121?" Vipul asked

"Not now, I sure will tell you all of it after I run some more tests for verification."

"You have been telling since yesterday that Sevugan is the source of infection for amma and appa. What is your new finding that makes you more confident now?"

"That our case is not incidental. I have been having a hunch for the last two days, but I have more data now. It is no longer a hunch. It was first amma and appa. Then the confirmation that Sevugan has been hacked. Then the curious case of Vani. That gave me more confidence in my theory. Then the information that Pankaj and Kamala's mother-in-law both were infected and both were using Robogenius NGN robots. One could be incidental, and two difficult but possible. 100 cannot be incidental. Now I have 100 samples to prove my hunch. That is my new data support."

"Hold On. You suspected that Pankaj and Kamala's robots were compromised. Did you get it confirmed?"

"Yes. Nothing to worry when Vanaja is there. She messaged me that honeypot was installed in both the robots and both did not respond to simulation, meaning both were compromised"

"So, Sevugan is compromised and similarly Pankaj and Kamala's robots were also compromised. Do you mean to say that all these robots connected to infection cases are robogenius robots and all these robots have been compromised" Vipul raised the relevant question.

"Could be, rather should be. Good line of thought and that is why I always like bouncing my thoughts with you, arguing with you" Vinitha complimented and Vipul beamed wide. I am sure that all the 100 of the Covid2121 infected people had an NGN robot in their house. We now need to find out if all these have been attacked. I can find that out easily with the help of my team"

"This piece of information would interest you, Vipul. 100 samples of Covid2121 infections taken by me belong to 40 families. There is a strong family connection in infection and almost all these 40 families have an NGN robot" Vinitha explained her line of thought.

Vinitha called her contact once again with a request to check if they were all from Robogenius.

After a short while, Vinitha shouted from her office room, at the top of her voice. "Thank you, Vipul, thank you. Our leads are taking us in the right direction. All those 40 NGN robots have been purchased from Robogenius."

"Is the government having data about the brand of the robot as well?"

"Yes, every data possible. Data intelligent country."

"You had another hunch. Would the government have data if all these 40 robots have been attacked?" Vipul asked

"Possible if each one of them reported to CERT-In. CERT-In maintains a database of all security incidents and I can find out from the database. But we will not find anything there as the owners would still not be aware that their robots have been attacked. This attacker is very smart and did not leave any sign or log of the attack. Unlikely that anyone would have reported" Vinitha explained.

"How do we find out then?" Vipul was worried.

"I will ask my office to find out that information. If information is not available, we have to prepare the information" Vinitha smiled.

"Assuming that your logic is correct, where is the first infection in a family coming from, if the lockdown is very effective?"

"One person may not have followed the lockdown guidelines properly and could have become the source for others in the family."

"Does not sound logical at all. How come the lockdown is effective overall but not effective for one person from each family? Moreover, what is that connection with NGN robots, that too from Robogenius, for all these 40 samples?"

"I am getting confused about that."

"I have now asked my team to analyse the data for 5,00,000 infected cases in India. We will know for sure."

"It must be very complex. How long will it take to analyse 5,00,000?"

"Very easy. Once the model is built, it is just a question of feeding the data and reports would start coming in minutes." Vinitha started mapping all the information she knew in a mindmap. "We got lots of information, that too seemingly unconnected information and strongly connected inferences. They are all falling in line, as you said"

"I am not seeing any line" Vipul looked at her mindmap

"Read the flow now and you will see a clear connection" Vinitha showed him her map.

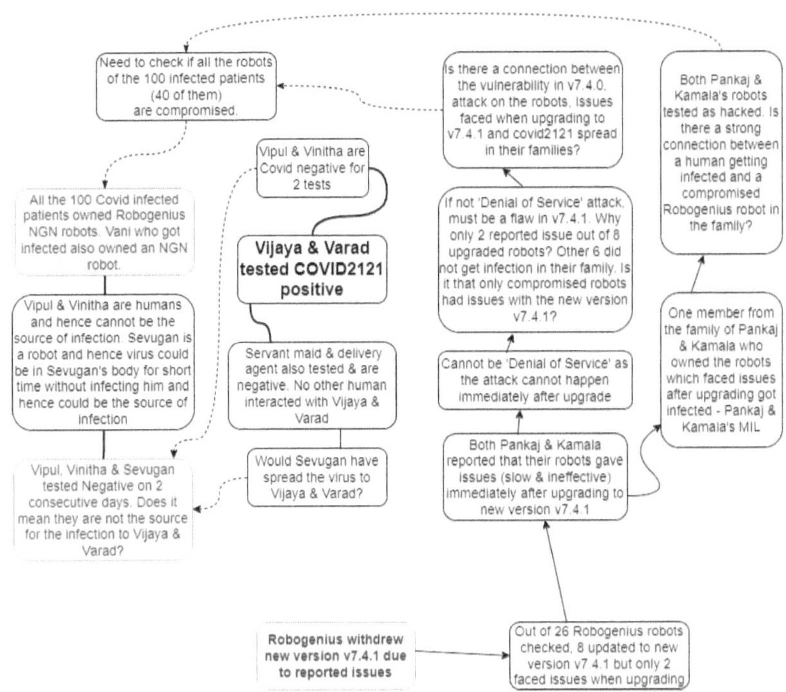

Vipul started scratching his head and Vinitha moved away before he could understand the mindmap.

She called her CEO from her phone and said, "I need the special privilege pass for my car and I am coming to the office. Can you organize to establish a Covid2121 test lab in my office? I need instant results for the various tests I am going to conduct. Also, please get some medical professionals to be available for support".

"Why do you need medical professional?"

"I want advice on Covid2121 and more importantly how to test a robot's skin for the presence of virus" Vinithia replied but her CEO could not understand and appreciate.

"Please organize a sound technical team of a minimum of five people as a special task force as well. Last but not the least, I am coming with my house robot. He will be in the office for the next two days. Please arrange necessary permissions for my house robot."

"Why do you need your robot? If it is for supplying tea, coffee and snacks, we have enough robots in the office. You don't need to bring yours." Her boss was puzzled.

"No. I need my Sevugan only. I will tell you why after I reach the office." Vinitha put her phone down and started getting ready to go to the office.

When Vinitha came out of her room, Vipul was astonished to see her dress.

"Anti-viral dress. This dress rejects all virus particles. Need to take care to cover my entire body, especially my hands. Hands are the most common carriers for Covid2121. It mainly spreads through the hands of the infected people. Hands pick up virus particles and they stay on the hand for 30 minutes." Vinitha gave a big explanation.

Sevugan came out of the kitchen carrying Vinitha's lunch.

"I don't need lunch". Vinitha sprayed a liberal dose of hand sanitizer on Sevugan's hands.

Sevugan asked, "Why should I come with you? To run a Covid2121 test on me daily?"

Vinitha did not have the patience to explain to him and instead came close to him and took his hands and said, "Please Sevugan, I want your support and it is very important. You are going to be a part of a globally important project. You will become famous soon." Vinitha said with a big smile.

"Then it is fine. I am coming. Don't leave me." Sevugan ran behind Vinitha.

"That is better. I told you managing an NGN robot is akin to managing an intelligent employee in your team." Vipul commented.

"Whether she would crack Covid2121 mystery or not, my wife learnt how to manage next generation robots." Vipul was happy.

Just when Vinitha opened the main door to go out, *Abra* switched on the screen with a Red Alert briefing message.

Vinitha and Sevugan also came inside to hear the Red Alert news briefing.

Dr. Lobo came on the screen wearing a Covid2121 special mask and started interacting with the viewers.

"Covid2121 infections are continuing to increase. But we are confident that separation will bring down the spread. We are also researching if the virus can spread through animals. It does not seem to be so, but we are checking all possibilities"

"Lockdown announced by the PM is expiring the day after tomorrow. I thought he will make some announcements about the lockdown. Whether the lockdown is getting extended or not." Vipul was disappointed.

"They will announce it the day after tomorrow. What is the hurry?" Vinitha smiled.

"Dr. Lobo started thinking but is on the wrong track." Vinitha said when leaving.

"How can you be confident that he is wrong? He is a world-renowned scientist," Vipul asked.

"Because I have the power of data to disprove his theory and Sevugan would not like him to be labelled as an animal."

"For sure, we are built with six senses and cannot be equated to animals." Sevugan spurted out immediately. He moved out ready to go.

Vipul pulled Vinitha aside and asked in a whisper. "So, you are sure that robogenius robots spread the virus to humans? Why don't you call and talk to Dr. Lobo about this? He will be able to give you better inputs."

"Will do, but I need to do some tests before that. I am looking for at least one positive test on Sevugan." Vinitha left, followed by Sevugan.

FRIDAY, 25ᵀᴴ APRIL 2121

There was no message from Vinitha until that evening. Vipul kept pinging Vinitha on her phone but she did not respond.

Vipul was alone at home, and it was boring to kill the time, especially with the anxiety about Vinitha's investigation on Covid2121. Though he was not fully convinced of her postulates, he was amazed at the confidence and boldness of his wife in challenging established scientists like Vittal. He slept on the sofa watching a movie after lunch.

He was woken up by the ringing of his hand phone. Vipul pressed the Answer button and asked, "Vinu. What happened? Why were you silent for so long? I am waiting for your call."

"OK. What happened to your Covid2121 investigation?"

"There are some interesting updates. Will update you when I reach home."

"And when will that be? Did you manage to test Sevugan?"

"Not once, multiple tests but all the tests ended up negative. We now have test results over a period of 24 hours and all tests are negative. I was waiting for the 24-hour time window to get over."

"Did you take all the tests on his palms?"

"No. I am not so dumb. We managed to test on all possible body parts but still could not get even one positive test result."

"What happened to your hunch then? So, Sevugan is not the source of infection?"

"Not necessarily. I still will not rule it out. I am missing something and not able to figure out at this stage." Vinitha disconnected the call.

Vinitha came home finally tagged along by Sevugan by 6 PM.

Vinitha was looking very tired and was not showing any interest in talking to Vipul. But Vipul could not control his curiosity.

"Are you sure about your theory that Sevugan was the source of infection to amma and appa?"

"95%."

"How?"

"I told you yesterday that data of 100 infected people cannot be incidental. Now I have the data of 5,00,000 infected people in India and the results show the same trend."

"Which means?"

"Of the 5,00,000 infected patients, 95% have an NGN robot. Too high to be incidental, and 5,00,000 patients are from 2,90,000 families, same trend."

"What is the overall % of NGN robots?"

"28% of total robots in the world are NGN robots."

"That looks like a strong case in favour of your hypothesis. Deviation cannot be so huge."

"Did you check the other angle, i.e., how many of these 2,90,000 robots are Robogenius robots?"

"We went a step further. We tested the NGN robots of a few of the Covid2121 victims. We have tested 35 robots, so far, and all of them are Robogenius robots and all these robots have been attacked. This cannot be incidental. There is a link between infection and Robogenius robots for sure and possibly all are attacked Robogenius robots".

"This supports our hypothesis." Vipul involuntarily changed over to 'our hypothesis'.

"Why don't you reach out to Robogenius to ask for additional info about the exploit code Vanaja talked about?"

"We made multiple attempts but could not extract any response."

"Not surprising. They are 'numero uno' in robotics. I am proud that an Indian company is 'numero uno'" Vipul clarified.

"That is fine. It is ok if they don't respond to enquiries about products and technology. This is a matter of public interest. We know how to make them respond"

"What do you plan to do now?"

"My CEO made one last attempt this morning. He messaged Mr. Vinod Sharma that there is some strong evidence available with us linking Robogenius with Covid2121 and we are obliged to report the findings to CERT-In[1]".

"Did he get a response from Robogenius?"

"He got a response that Mr. Vinod Sharma will contact me today once he is free."

"I am very tired. If you keep asking me questions, I will sleep even while talking to you."

"One last question. What happened to your plans of hacking, unethically hacking government records, with an ethical motive, of course?"

"Decided not to."

---

[1] CERT-In - Computer Emergency Response Team, India. Government team responsible for cyber security incident reporting and analysis.

"Why? Hope I am not the reason for the change of mind. I already agreed to support your plan." Vipul was worried that he should not be blamed later.

"I decided to remain ethical, adhering to the principles of ethical hacking."

"What made you change your decision?"

"Multiple reasons. The decision was taken when I was depressed. Now I am in *high spirits*. I decided to stay fair to my professional ethics. More importantly, I am now more confident that we will get back our license very soon anyway." Vinitha smiled. Vipul understood and was enthralled with her confidence.

Vipul wanted to ask her lots of things, about the RTPCR tests on Sevugan. How did they test Sevugan? How did he become negative if he was the carrier to Vijaya, Varad, etc.? But he did not want to disturb her sleep. He kept peeping inside the bedroom every 15 minutes to see if she was awake.

She had to be woken up in an hour anyway to answer an important call came on her phone.

"Vinu. Get up, Vinod Sharma is on the phone and he wants to talk to you. He is asking me to wake you up even if you are sleeping. He says it is very urgent."

"Who is Vinod Sharma?" Vinitha was half asleep.

"He is the CEO of world-famous Robogenius. Dumbo. Which world are you in? You must be one of the few privileged ones in the world for Vinod Sharma to call you. He is the second richest person in the world now."

"He may be the second richest man in the world and I am an ordinary citizen. But he knows this call is very important for him as well. Otherwise, he would not have called" Vinitha got up and went to the bathroom.

"Robogenius. That is great. The CEO of Robogenius is waiting for you on the call. I cannot believe it. I had sent him multiple emails for an appointment, but he did not respond to any of my emails." Vipul was excited and was waiting outside the bathroom talking excitedly. Their conversation was flowing across the bathroom door.

"Would he reveal the suspense we are all waiting for??"

"I have no idea."

"Can I also participate in the call? It is a virtual call anyway." Vipul requested.

Vinitha did not respond.

Vinod Sharma sounded as well as looked like a business nerd even on the *shadverse* screen.

"I am sorry, I slept as I was very tired." Vinitha opened the conversation.

"It is OK. I can understand. You must be exhausted. I heard a lot about your work from your CEO."

"Do you have answers for my questions?" Vinitha was brusque and straight to the topic.

"Yes. I have my R&D Head, Veer Sundar also with me. Shoot."

"Can a robot, especially an NGN robot be affected by a virus?"

"Don't joke madam. We did not come to this meeting to listen to your jokes." Veer jumped to answer before Vinod could answer.

"Professor, I am asking a question. I am not suggesting anything. Please just answer the questions. I know that it is not possible. I wanted to hear from the experts and I am not an expert in Robotics." Vinitha gave it back. Her biggest strength was *calling a spade a spade.* Vinitha's age, gender and her friendly looks were a problem for her many times. People take time to give her due respect.

"Virus requires cells to replicate. Even NGN humanoid robots do not have any biological component." Veer seemed to have understood Vinitha. At least he couldn't pooh-pooh her. She was no ordinary woman.

"I read that the NGN robot's skin is made of a material equivalent to that of human skin. Can a virus infect the robot's skin?"

"Curious question. NGN robot's skin is a chemical component to give the look and feel and characteristics similar to that of human skin, but it is not a biological component like human skin. For example, the NGN robot's skin cannot sweat. Will not have hair growth. Blood will not ooze if cut, will not have boils, etc. The only connection from this skin to other components of the robot are the touch sensors placed at convenient places and the virus cannot travel through the sensors. The virus requires cells to infect." Veer explained, very patiently now.

"Are you saying that it is impossible for a virus to stay and replicate in any of the components of a robot?"

"One hundred percent."

Vipul thought, "Veer must have studied and worked in the USA."

"OK. Can a virus stay in the skin of the robot for some time?"

"We never thought about this possibility. I could not immediately answer this question when Vinod asked me this morning. I simulated and tested the same in our test lab. Yes. The virus can stay on the skin of an NGN robot but cannot spread to any other part of the NGN robot." Veer explained.

"That is interesting. What are the possible options by which the NGN robot's skin gets the virus?"

"Same as a human. If an NGN robot touches any surface where the virus was there or a person is infected with the virus, virus particles can stay on in the skin of the robot but only for a maximum of one hour. The virus will become ineffective after one hour."

"I understand that a human can get a virus by touching a surface with the virus as well as through air if a person is at close distance with the infected person even if there is no touch. Can a robot acquire the virus through the air?"

"Not possible. A robot cannot acquire a virus through the air even if it is in close proximity to an infected human. Not possible at all. A robot does not need breathing and a robot does not eat anything. The only possibility, if at all, is by touching a surface with the virus."

"Can a robot get the virus from another robot with the virus?"

"Possible, but again only through touch."

"Thanks, professor. That is all I want to know. I read many of these from the Internet but wanted to hear from the *horse's mouth*. And you have given me some new points to think about." Vinitha gave a big *namaste* to Veer.

"Vinitha, you wanted to find out from Sir about the exploit code. Did you forget?" Vipul was worried that Vinitha forgot about the attack on Sevugan. Vinitha is not of the type to forget.

"Yes. Sir, I have been asking your team to share information about your buggy patch version 7.4.1 but I did not receive any response" Vinitha opened the discussion.

"I don't know why you want that information. The patch has nothing to do with Covid2121 virus. Anyway, I will share whatever info we have."

"That is more than sufficient, sir. Thanks for your support."

"Shoot your questions."

"Your press conference mentioned that a bug was reported on 7.4.1 from the customers. I could not get any more info. What is the bug and how was the bug identified? When was the bug noticed?"

"The first report was on 12th April 2121."

"When was 7.4.1 released?"

"12th April 2121."

"So, you received the complaint as soon as the new version was released. Also, you received an error report two days before the first Covid2121 was reported."

"Could be. But why are you connecting the two? What is the connection? Do you mean to say that Covid2121 happened because we released a new OS? Sounds ridiculous!"

"I don't know at this stage. OK. What was the reported bug?"

"We designed the NGN robots in such a way that they dump diagnostic information to our SOC[2] team whenever there is an anomaly so that our SOC team can work on the diagnostics."

"OK. What is the definition of an anomaly?"

"Events such as anomalous behaviour of the robot, intrusion attempts, critical errors, etc. We keep this option as a safety for the users without intruding into their time or privacy."

"I understand. What was the event reported on 12th April 2121?"

---

[2] SOC – Security Operations Center, the team responsible for monitoring security alerts in real time so that action can be taken immediately

"There were continuous error reports and diagnostic dumps to our SOC. But while analysing the log, the error details were not there in any of the diagnostic dumps. Because of the continuous dump, the robots became very slow and ineffective."

"Interesting. What action did your SOC team take?"

"Our incident analysis function is offshored to Bangladesh. We checked with our incident analysis team. They could not get any valuable information about the error. They suspected it to be a 'Distributed Denial of Service Attack' on our SOC."

"Very interesting. Did these alerts stop after reverting to v7.4.0?"

"Yes. We are not getting any error logs after reverting to the older patch. We thought the problem was identified to be a new vulnerability unknowingly added in 7.4.1 code and closed the Root Cause report."

"Did you check if all the robots which got upgraded to 7.4.1 reported the dump to your SOC?"

"We did not check. We never thought about it"

"It is hard to believe that a world-famous robotics company would not check this simple point ie whether the problem was reported from all the robots or only few robots" Vinitha looked straight at the eyes of Vinod Sharma.

"What are you trying to hint at? Are you saying that we are hiding something?" Vinod raised his voice.

Vinitha was not to be perturbed. "I did not say anything like that. I am only explaining whatever I know and trying to get answers from you for whatever I don't know. I did not start any blame. Why are you feeling that you are hiding something?" Vinitha kept her cool.

"OK. I answered all your questions. What more?" Vinod's tone was unfriendly.

"Don't you want to know that not all the robots which got upgraded to 7.4.1 did not face the problem. Only those robots which were **already attacked** before the version upgrade faced the issue" Vinitha said it in slow but in a clear tone and looked at the face of Vinod and Veer. She specifically gave the stress to the words 'already attacked'. She tried to read their expression. They were clearly stumped but she could not read anything beyond that.

"How do you know?" Vinod's tone was meek. He never faced a lady like Vinitha and he liked her boldness.

"Because I personally tested 30 of your robots and collected the exploit code" Vinitha paused "and we sent the code to your office and asking for a response from your office. We could have solved Covid2121 riddle by now if only your team responded in time"

"Sorry. Nobody reported this to me, believe me" Vinitha could not check if Vinod was truthful. Good quality thot-pad could detect if the statement is true or not but this was not the time to conduct 'lie detector' tests.

"How could so many robots could get compromised?" Veer chipped in.

"I understand that 7.4.1 was released to fix a 'Remote Code Execution' vulnerability in v7.4.0. That means all NGN robots were vulnerable to 'Remote Code Execution' during the intervening period."

"Unfortunately, yes. Please don't report this to CERT-In. Consumers will lose faith in our robots. We came to know of the vulnerability in 7.4.0 and released the fix quickly. Unfortunately, the new release backfired. We are still not able to identify any bug with the earlier 7.4.1 code released." Vinod explained.

"Yes, sir. You are correct. My presumption is that v7.4.1 fixed the vulnerability and the attempts to exploit that vulnerability in a compromised robot when the vulnerability was not there in v7.4.1 showed up as error dumps to your SOC. Unfortunately, you stopped your research assuming it was a bug. Tendency to do a quick fix." Vinitha explained.

"Strange behaviour. How are you sure of your statement?" Veer questioned.

"Because I tested few robots which reported issue with v7.4.1 and all of them showed *indicators of compromise*[3]. I thought you would share more light on this" Vinitha smiled

---

[3] Indicators of compromise - forensic evidence of potential intrusions on a system or network

"Good thinking, madam. We never thought about this aspect. But the attempt cannot come from so many robots. That is why we were paranoid. Veer, why don't you explore this angle?"

Veer hesitantly said, "Sure". His 'sure' sounded like unsure surely. He was apparently not happy to listen to lessons from a young lady.

"OK. You released the updated 7.4.1 code a couple of days back and this seems to be running without any problem. What did you fix in the new version which made it work well?"

"Nothing. We just added a control to stop spurious error reports to the SOC. We added a limit on excessive error dumps and added an artificial intelligence code to stop error reporting if the error log did not include useful information. That solved the problem." Veer explained.

"Essentially, you stopped the reporting instead of tracing the root cause of the reporting" Vinitha looked at Veer with a confident look and Veer had to instantly down his face.

"Did you trace the root cause of the excessive error dumps?"

"I already told you that the log did not have any information. It looked to be a spurious error report." Veer was getting restless with the questioning.

"It does not look spurious to me. I did research and found out that not all robots that upgraded to 7.4.1 faced the problem. Only a small percentage of those upgraded to 7.4.1 faced the issue. I have the numbers and I can quote them." Vinitha explained.

"Not required, madam. That is normal. Only those robots that faced some errors encountered the problem. It is not necessary that everyone with the new version would have to face the problem. I already explained to you that there was no bug in the new version." Veer clarified.

"Exactly. That is my point. It is not a bug in the code. It does not look like a 'Denial of Service' attack either as your SOC would have received attack details if it is an attack. It appears to me that the robots which showed the issue after upgrading to the new version were already compromised and the new version apparently created a logjam in the compromised robots as it removed the vulnerability for the compromise. It fixed the vulnerability but the robots were already compromised when the patch got loaded and hence reported excessive error dumps, but the compromise was so intelligent that all attack details have been removed during the attack. This is my presumption but a strong possibility." Vinitha explained.

Veer was stunned and gave serious consideration to Vinitha for the first time.

"Veer. Please set up a special team and work on this angle quickly. I want a report on this tomorrow." Vinod instructed.

"Vinod ji, I am a big fan of your robots. We use your NGN robot in our house." Vipul was waiting for his turn to speak to Vinod.

"Not only you, Mr. Vipul. Our robots are used in 72 countries. We are the Number 1 robot vendor in 72 countries." Vinod was proud.

"I know. That is why I confidently selected your robot for our requirement, and we are very happy with our Sevugan." Vipul went on.

"Wait a minute, Vipul. How many countries did you say, Vinod ji? How are you very confident about this number? You could be operating in more countries."

"No madam. We operate only from 72 countries. We exited from some markets as these markets were not profitable for us. But why are you so particular about this number?"

"Yes. The number 72 is still in my mind very firmly, because Covid2121 is in my mind firmly for the past one week and Covid2121 infections are reported from 72 countries as per the last news report. Let us match the countries where you are popular and the list of 72 countries from where Covid2121 infections were reported."

Vinod was astonished at Vinitha's sharpness and grasp. "Smart young lady." Vinod said aloud.

"You have a high-priority notification, and do you want to open the message?" Vinitha's phone interrupted and Vinitha saw a highlighted message from Vanaja. She instantly opened the message and said, "Another interesting info as breaking news."

"You are breaking us very badly with so many discoveries in such a short time." Vinod appeared nervous.

Vinitha shared the screen with everyone. It was a set of graphs showing the number of reported infections plotted against geographies, NGN robots, etc. One graph showed the number of robots from Robogenius.

Vinitha explained, "I asked my team to collect data on the 5,00,000 Covid infections globally, 93% of them use an NGN robot and out of these NGN robots, 98.5% of the robots are from Robogenius."

"Of course. Robogenius is the most popular robot maker and we have the largest market share of NGN robots anyway." Vinod countered.

"OK. What is your market share in NGN robots?"

"Around 76%."

"Still there is a huge difference between 76% and 98.5%."

"What are you trying to say?"

"I first got the confirmation that there is a strange connection between Covid2121 infections and NGN robots and now an additional inference, even stronger connection between Covid2121 and NGN robots from Robogenius."

"Are you blaming that Robogenius is responsible for Covid2121? That is not a good idea. Especially if it is not substantiated. We will not take it lightly, as this will dent our image. I did not give you all this information only to realize that you are working hard to defame us."

"I am not suggesting. My job is to put the data, rationale and inferences. Let the experts make the conclusion. Don't jump to conclusions. Listen to one more interesting analysis from my resourceful friend Vanaja" Vinitha smiled.

There was pin-drop silence in the call. Vinitha waited for few minutes and showed another graph and said "She tested 100 of the Robogenius robots in the house of the infected patients and can you guess the number of robots which were found to be compromised"

Nobody could afford to respond.

"All 100 of them were found to be compromised. Is this not enough proof for my theory" Vinitha concluded.

"I quickly checked the list of countries from where Covid2121 infections were reported and the list of countries where Robogenius is popular." Vipul had to share his part of the responsibility.

"What does it say?"

"Both the lists match 100%."

Vinod was startled by further and further incriminating data. "Are you planning to report?"

"Yes. I have to report to CERT-In."

"How would you report to CERT-In based on possibilities? We still do not have 'Indicators of Compromise'. I will ask Veer and his team to find the IOCs and we will ourselves report after finding out all necessary information" Vinod raised his voice a bit.

"My house robot has been attacked. I have proof." Vinitha also raised her voice.

"Do you have the *attack vector*[4] and *indicators of compromise*[5]?"

"No, because the attacker deleted all *forensic*[6] information by exploiting the vulnerability. We could not find any trace. The same thing would have happened when you released the 7.4.1 version for the first time. The new version removed the vulnerability and found something wrong but could not get any log details to dump to SOC. You are aware of that." Vinitha explained calmly.

"That means it is still a possibility only, if not an assumption. CERT-In will not accept assumptions." Vinod countered.

"No. I have clear proof that the attack happened."

"How can you be sure? You said you don't have any forensic information."

"I collected *wireshark*[7] logs and found out that my robot is sending malicious traffic to its console software."

---

[4] Attack vector - Pathway or method used by an attacker to access a network or system (robot) in an attempt to exploit known vulnerabilities.

[5] Indicators of Compromise (IOC) - Information that indicates a system (robot) might have been attacked and information inferred from the attack. Reporting the IOC helps the community to implement safeguards so that the attack does not happen in their systems.

[6] (Digital) Forensic – Evidence to prove a digital crime and the traces in the investigation of the crime.

[7] Wireshark – Application used to capture network traffic for analysis.

"That is absurd. A robot has to send traffic to the base console software. How could it be controlled otherwise?" Veer intervened.

"I am aware of that Mr. Veer. I am not an idiot to suggest that robots should not communicate with the console software. We have seen that this communication is nothing to do with regular control information."

"What does it communicate then?"

"We are not able to decode that and that is why we want your help."

"Send it to us then instead of reporting to CERT-In. Why did you not send it to us?" Veer tried intimidation.

"We had, and we are still waiting for your response. You did not respond to our attempts. This is the first time we have got a response from anyone in Robogenius. We tried multiple times, and multiple channels. This is not something you would want us to send to your help desk on a normal mail, would you? We could have done that of course, and it would have gone to too many people in your own organisation. And you know what could have happened." Vinitha was used to intimidation. Now she was dishing out some.

"OK. Send the details and wireshark dump to Veer. He will find out. We shall decide about reporting to CERT-In after Veer finds out the indicators of compromise." Vinod adopted a conciliatory tone.

"Sorry, sir. It is my obligation to report to CERT-In. It is a regulatory provision to report all attacks within 12 hours of knowing the attack." Vinitha said calmly.

"But you still don't have the indicators of compromise." Vinod protested.

"Please read the provision, Mr. Vinod. I don't need to give the indicators of compromise to CERT-In. I am very confident that my robot has been compromised and it is my social obligation and professional ethics to report it. That is what the law of the land also mandates."

"I know enough about the law. We are aware of the laws of 72 countries. I am only suggesting that let us not go to the authorities with half-baked information." Vinod understood it was hard to intimidate Vinitha.

"CERT-In expects and wants details even if it is half-baked information, Sir. The idea of CERT-In is not regulatory obligation. The objective here is proactive control to limit the spread of the threat. They need information as soon as anyone knows any information about an attack."

Vinod and Veer could not respond. "Madam, we are aware of our social obligations. We are a giant organisation, and we spend 15% of our revenue on cyber security. We give away huge money on bug bounty. We gave Rs. 50 lakhs to the person who reported to us about the 'Remote Code Execution' vulnerability in 7.4.0. We do give serious attention to cyber security. I am sure we should be able to reward you profusely for all your efforts to help us with this vulnerability. You have done a great job for us. Give us your wireshark logs and we will take care. Don't worry. We will recognize you with a huge bug bounty." Vinod was aware of the *sama, dana, bheda* and *danda*[8] strategy.

Vinitha smiled. Vinod could not make out if his strategy was working or not.

"Veer, this madam seems to be very smart and knowledgeable. We should use her for our ongoing third-party vulnerability assessments." Vinod added.

"Thanks for your compliments, sir. I would be too happy to take up your work. I will inform my CEO right away after this call. He will be too happy and will talk to you about the possible new business. I will be happy to receive a bug bounty reward commensurate to my work" Vinod and Veer felt relieved that their strategy was working. Vinod knew that if *sama* does not work, *dana* will work for sure.

"But I must report to CERT-In before I inform my CEO about the new business opportunity. That is my professional ethics if not regulation." Vinitha added and smiled. Vinod and Veer were flabbergasted.

---

[8] Sama, dana, bheda and danda – Ancient Indian strategy for diplomacy which when translated would mean conciliation, giving money, divide and rule and punishment in that order to achieve an objective.

"Don't worry sir. CERT-In is not cyber police. Their objective is not to find fault for the attack. Their objective is to reduce and limit the attacks." Vinitha added.

"Thank you, Sirs. I know both of you are very busy and your time is precious. Especially now, since you know that something is seriously amiss. I shall send you all the details and wireshark logs. Please message your email IDs in this chat window and I will send them in 15 minutes. I would be happy if you can update me your findings on the attack details" Vinitha offered a genuine *namaste* before disconnecting the call.

After disconnecting the call, Vinitha called her boss and briefed him about her discussion with Vinod and Veer and requested him to pass on the confirmation to the Health Ministry.

Her boss asked, "Are you sure? We will be crucified if we are not able to prove our hypothesis."

"It is no longer a hypothesis. I have a concrete rationale."

"You are still calling it **rationale** and not **proof.**"

"Yes. I have to be politically correct. As you said, I will be crucified otherwise. If you want, I can prepare the incident analysis report with the information I have and the inferences which you can send to the Health Ministry." Vinitha offered.

"That is a good idea. Please prepare and send me. I will send an alert message to the Health Secretary. He will sure lend his ear to us."

"Let him. Otherwise, he will be doing great injustice to mankind." Vinitha disconnected the call and locked herself in her office room to prepare the report. She slept in the room after sending the report to her boss.

SATURDAY, 26ᵀᴴ APRIL 2121

Vipul was excited. "Vinu, get up. There is an interesting news."

"What is that great news which cannot wait? Why cannot you allow me to sleep peacefully?" Vinitha gets irritated if someone disturbs her when she is dreaming.

Vinitha was dreaming that a robot was chasing her on the road, and she was running fast crying, "This robot is spreading the virus. Please help! Please help! Arrest the robot!" Vinitha stopped and looked at the robot. The face looked very familiar to her and then she shouted, "Sevugan, what are you doing? Why are you in deceit?"

Vinitha got up and started laughing. Vipul was puzzled at her strange behaviour. Vinitha narrated her dream and Vipul also laughed.

"This stupid virus and that stupid robot are taking a toll on you. Take a break from your stupid investigation." Vipul said imitating Vinitha's style.

"My investigation is not a stupid investigation. It is a systematic & logical problem-solving process."

"True. Your investigation has already reached news channels. You are in the Top 10 news this morning."

"Oh, God. What are you saying? It is not good at all. Vinod Sharma is already upset with me. He will think that I leaked the information. Who would have leaked the info to news channels?"

"Our news channels would not broadcast information sent to them. They know how to sniff for sensational info. You are in the 'Breaking News' just as we speak. Your phone is continuously ringing and here you are dreaming about robots."

When Vinitha came down to the living room, Sevugan was standing and watching the news and said, "Madam has become famous overnight. But I don't like her getting famous by blaming us as the reason for Covid spread."

"Breaking News. As per our latest report published first in our news channel, robots are spreading the Covid2121 virus. A cyber security specialist from Chennai is suggesting that all the Covid2121 infections happened because of robots. She has suggested to the health minister to switch off all the robots to contain Covid2121. The Health Minister is evaluating the veracity of her claim."

"When did I suggest switching off the robots?   Are they suggesting that I am suffering from amnesia? I don't remember ever telling anyone to switch off the robots, not even in the report." Vinitha was furious. "The saving grace is that the news did not mention anything about Robogenius." Vinitha added. She paused. Is it possible that they have engineered the news to create panic among the people? That robots have to be switched off? What a horrible thing to do?" She was fuming. As usual, it became Vipul's job to reason with her.

"Vinu, you are jumping to conclusions. It is unprofessional to presume that that they leaked the info"

"But who else does it benefit? Nowhere is the information about the vulnerability in Robogenius robots or their incomplete research mentioned."

"I agree my genius. But you are getting distracted. Your job is to focus on the virus. Not on their viciousness, even if it is so."

"You are right. I shall ignore the news and the nonsense. I will focus on my job. Please help me by being my own 'firewall' from all this."

The news switched over to a debate or rather an argument between four people with two people supporting her claim and two others arguing that it is an absurd claim.

"How did these people manage to understand and come to conclusion on such a complex and lengthy report in just five minutes? It took me a week of investigation and five hours of report writing to prepare the report." Vinitha was even more furious.

Within five minutes, the debate went into mayhem. A smiling, charming, bespectacled stout facilitator stopped talking when both sides went into heated arguments.

Vinitha's phone rang with a priority alert tone, "Call from my CEO." Vinitha answered the call.

"Did you report to CERT-In Vinitha?" The CEO came to the topic directly.

"Not yet, sir. I wanted to do it yesterday itself but was busy preparing the report for you and slept after that."

"Good. Don't do it then. Vinod is very upset. He called me and said that you reported to CERT-In despite him requesting you to wait for further investigation. He thought that you had already reported on seeing the news reports this morning."

"I did not report or leak it to anyone, but I need to report now."

"Please don't report. Vinod is promising us huge business and that will take us to great heights."

"But it is a regulatory requirement and obligation to report, Sir."

"But it did not happen to our company. Why should the company lose a big business opportunity for something which did not even happen to the company?"

"Sure. I will not report it in the name of our company. But I must report the attack on our house robot. If that suits you, I will ask my husband to report in his name as an attack on the house robot."

"I would not recommend that as well." The CEO knew that it was not that easy to pressurize Vinitha.

Just then the calling bell rang. The image from the video door phone gets transferred to the wallboard when there is a bell push as a 'Picture in Picture'. That can interrupt the ongoing call as well. Vipul screamed, "Vittal Lobo has been called for the argument. We can expect some sensible comments from Dr. Lobo."

"*Arre nahin yaar.* Dr. Lobo is standing at our door. Go and open the door." Vinitha shouted.

"Sir, it seems Dr. Lobo has come to our house. Will talk to him and call you back Sir, if you don't mind."

"OK. Be careful dealing with Lobo. I will come if you want." The CEO knew that Vinitha was very smart but was always worried about her diplomatic, rather undiplomatic, skills.

"Yesterday Vinod Sharma and today Vittal Lobo." Vipul was excited.

"It must be a very important development if he has come directly to our home to meet Vinitha in the midst of his busy schedule."

"Otherwise, people like Vittal don't come knocking on doors unannounced." Vipul opened the door and escorted Dr. Lobo to the living room.

Vinitha freshened up quickly and went to the meeting room. "I am sorry to keep you waiting. I was shocked to watch some stupid comments in the news ascribed to me. Was it too long?"

Vittal neither stood up nor offered his hand. Vinitha knew that Covid2121 protocol did not permit a handshake. But something about his demeanour told her that this was not the reason for his unfriendliness. He could have gotten up from the sofa and offered a *namaste* especially since he was meeting a lady for the first time. Vinitha was not sure if it was a sign of arrogance that he was a world-renowned scientist and much sought-after government official for the past week.

Vinitha assessed him. She normally assesses the body language of all her professional contacts. That gives her an edge in the discussion. He gave her a typical scientist look but a tired look as well. He must be in his late fifties. Why should all the scientists sport a beard, that too salt & pepper beard? This is perhaps a fashion statement for scientists.

Vinitha could sense a feeling of disappointment in his eyes. He must have expected an elderly, white-haired and bespectacled lady. She gave a sigh that she could not help.

"No problem. I must say sorry. I was to meet you tomorrow morning but managed to get answers to some of your questions and hence was curious to know more about your hunches."

"They are not hunches anymore." Vinitha raised her voice. Vinitha never allowed anyone to underestimate her, even if it was a world-renowned scientist. She did not care.

"We scientists consider everything as hunches unless proved beyond doubt. That is the difference between scientists and engineers." Vittal smiled.

"I have lots of rationale for my theory. I am just looking for that one conclusive evidence." Vinitha did not give up.

"Did you manage to get a positive test on any robot, so far?" Vittal retorted.

"No. That is the problem. I am still waiting."

"Then your theory is still a hunch. We will upgrade it to theory once you get one robot tested positive." Vittal smiled. "And the chances are very less." He added.

"I know your reputation as a top scientist. I am sure that you cannot appreciate my findings being a scientist." Vinitha used sweet sarcasm all through. "But you agree with me unconsciously, at least a teeny-weeny bit. You would not have come all the way to Chennai otherwise." Vinitha smiled.

"OK. Let us come to the point. Explain to me your rationale." Vittal quizzed with perhaps real interest.

"By the way, I want to synch my contact card with yours. Would you like to accept?" Vittal opened his palm. Vinitha knew that he was a little more comfortable now.

Vinitha took her contact reader from her handbag and tied it around the top of her right ring finger. It was a small card, the size of a pumpkin seed. She pointed her finger at Vittal and said, "Synch contact".

She got the response instantly, "Contact synched. Updated new contact Vittal. Do you want to upload to your profile list?"

She said, "Yes."

"Under which category and under which nickname?"

"Official and Professor Virus." Vinitha smiled at Vittal.

"I am not Professor Virus, I am Professor Anti-virus." Vittal laughed aloud.

Vittal's contact reader was slightly bigger in size and it asked him a lot more questions before the contact was updated. He stored the new details as 'Vinitha Cyber' with a tag, "Young lady who infected her robot with a virus."

Vinitha told herself, I am used to ridicule and I will not allow it to affect me. On the outside, she smiled and said, "And infected me with her enthusiasm. I am sure you mean it, sir." Vittal was now convinced that she was no pushover. Despite her age and her simple looks.

"Tell me your **story**, madam." Vinitha thought he gave artificial stress for the word story. He shifted his stance to listen to her story. Vinitha was not sure if he was serious and if he would believe her theory. She was not sure if he had come because of the pressure from the health secretary based on her report sent the previous night. But she was very appreciative of the instant response from the Health Ministry and Vittal Lobo. How did they manage to make so much happen when she was sleeping?

"My inference is that, unlike Covid19, Covid2121 is a **robot to human** apart from possible **human to human."**

The professor was not startled. He must have been briefed sufficiently about Vinitha's report by the health secretary.

"You are not a medical professional, but you must be aware that a virus can survive and spread only in a biological body. A robot's body is full of mechanical and electronic components. Viruses cannot survive in mechanical and electronic components. A virus requires biological cells. I would have appreciated it if you said, 'animal to human'. There are incidents of the 'animal to human' virus. Your theory looks absurd to me."

"I have studied and understood virology 101 in the last week. It would be foolish of me to suggest that the virus spreads in robots. Hope you listened to my words carefully. I was saying that, unlike Covid19, **Covid2121 spreads through robots. Not in robots."**

"What is the difference? What are you trying to hint?"

"Robots should be acting as transient carriers of the virus. Is it not possible that virus particles can stay alive on a surface for about one hour? Is it not true?"

"Very much possible. Does not require great research. Viruses can stay alive in robots for one hour and can spread to humans if the human touches a robot when the virus particles are on the surface. My point is that viruses can never survive inside the body of a robot like they do in a human body."

"I understand that. I repeat. I never said that the virus infects robots."

"If a robot gets a virus on its outside body, it must have come from another human. It is then like a human with a virus touching any metallic surface. The virus will remain on the surface for a maximum of one hour. A robot can get a virus from an infected human. But that is not of any significance to our problem."

"My theory is that a robot gets the virus and spreads it to humans, but the robot does not get it from humans. I don't have scientific proof yet, but I am sure of my theory.

"How are you sure of this? Explain to me your deduction."

"Both my mother and father got infected with Covid2121. They are staying with us. They did not get the virus from any other human. They were in touch with only the two of us and both of us have not gotten infected, yet. You don't need to be worried. We have just tested yesterday. So obviously, they could have got it from only one other source, our house robot."

"Lot of assumptions without scientific base. They could have gotten the virus in many other ways even if they were not in contact with any other human. Contact with a human is not the only way Covid2121 spreads."

"I agree. I also thought the same initially. But listen to few more confirmed postulates before concluding. Very high % of infected patients had robots especially NGN robots from Robogenius at their home, to add to that 100 of the robots in the houses of infected patients were tested and confirmed to have been hacked" Vinitha finished in one sentence and looked up at Viital.

"I expected that you will not agree with me readily. It is not the deduction from one inference. I have data of 5,00,000 infected people and a house robot, that too NGN robot, caused the infection in most of the 5,00,000 incidents."

"**I am not talking in the air.**" Vinitha completed long speech. Dr. Lobo remained silent for long.

"OK. How do the robots get the virus if not from another human? What is your theory here?" It looked like Dr.Lobo was getting convinced finally.

"I still don't have that answer. I am still looking for a spark to find that out. I thought you can throw some light on that as a virologist."

"I can only tell you that the virus can stay in a robot's hand or body for a maximum period of one hour if the robot touches any surface with the virus. I did research and found out that 'next generation robots' are built with skin akin to that of a human and that material can pick up the virus and can stay on their skin for about one hour, not more than that. But this is applicable to humans as well. I cannot deduce how robots can be the source of viruses for humans. It is beyond my comprehension. That is your theory. You need to deduce that."

"It is a good input you gave just now that the skin of a 'next generation robot' can pick up viruses and can stay for a period of one hour. It spreads to humans from a robot's skin within that one hour."

"You then do test on your house robot. You will come to know."

"I did but the test turned out to be negative."

"I thought as much. You then have to ignore your hunch."

"As you said, the virus stays on the robot's skin only for one hour. We will get positive test results only when we test within that one hour when the virus is on the skin of the robot. How do we know when the robot would get the virus?"

"Hmm. Tough problem. Do multiple tests."

"I did test my robot every hour for 30 hours and all the test results turned out to be negative."

"That is then enough proof that your theory is not feasible, let us look for some other clue." Lobo got up giving an impression that it is end of their conversation.

He sat down again and asked "I have a problem. You told me that your house robot was the source of infection for your father and mother and they got infection on two different days"

"Yes. Two days gap in between" Vinitha wondered why he asked this question.

"As I mentioned, the virus in your house robot could stay on his skin for one hour only. How could he have remained as a source of infection on two different days? Not possible" Lobo looked at Vinitha's face for clues.

"This is a good question, Doctor. Let me think about it. The possibility is that the robot gets the environment in which it picks up the virus for one hour every day" Vinitha thought for some time and added "Because, this is the pattern not only in our family. Same thing happened for my friend Vani as well. Two different people got infected on two different days" Vinitha added.

"What is that environment?"

"I don't know **yet**. I asked your help to find that out."

"I feel the theory itself is absurd. I am not aware of any reason why a robot can get Covid2121 other than if it happens to touch any surface fresh with a virus. That is the only possible scientific explanation." Lobo stood up to leave. His face showed that he was not happy with the outcome of this meeting.

"That is the problem now. I am also not clear as to how the robot inherits viruses in a unique way not common to humans. But I am 100% sure that the infections come from robots and that too from compromised Robogenius robots. It is something to do with that stupid attack on Robogenius robots. Unfortunately,

Robogenius is not helping me with that information. I am sure robots are taking the virus to humans and that is why the virus is spreading fast even during the lockdown. But I don't know how the robots are getting the virus."

"You may be logical. But as a scientist, I cannot agree with you unless you give me a scientific explanation."

"I would have revealed to you if I knew."

"Hmm. We are back to square one. I was told by the Health Secretary personally last night that you have an interesting new angle and I have been asked to focus on your theory. I could have scheduled a virtual meeting instead of flying all the way."

Vinitha was taken aback but that spurred her to anger. She never gives up. "Don't worry professor, you will get your answers by tomorrow morning. It is my promise that you will have all the answers by tomorrow."

"But why tomorrow morning? We can run all the necessary tests tonight if you want. The Prime Minister is expecting an answer from me tomorrow."

"Because I need to find that missing information from Robogenius. I will give another hard try today if I can get that information from Robogenius. I already sent them the log details. I would be happy if you can put pressure on Robogenius to come out with the details fast through the government".

Vittal did not comment and stood up to leave.

"Don't worry doctor. Your visit will not go waste. I will call you tomorrow with the answers." Vinitha gave a confident smile.

"OK. I believe you. I booked my return ticket to Delhi for tomorrow evening only. Call me once you get the answers. You have my number in your contacts now." Vittal walked out briskly.

Seeing Vittal leave, Vipul came into the living room.

"Why did the doctor leave so early, I thought you are going to be occupied for hours?" Vipul asked.

"He is not happy and does not want to agree with my theory."

"Does not matter. It is good anyway. I wanted to ask you a lot. Good that the professor left." Vipul laughed. He makes light of any situation. That is one positive trait in Vipul and Vinitha utilises that quite often thought not at that situation.

"It is not the right time for your positivity theory. Do you realize that I could be in big trouble if I don't solve this by tomorrow? I have just one day to absolve myself."

"I thought you are on *cloud nine*, your newfound status of meeting VVIPs like Dr. Lobo at our home and the popularity in news channels."

"Be serious Vipul. It is a double-edged weapon to move closely with people like Dr. Lobo. It could misfire as well. He is upset and believes strongly that I misled him with an absurd theory.

Dealing with such VVIPs comes with big risks as well. I would be put into big trouble if I don't get back to him with proof."

"OK. OK. Relax. What choice do we have now? What is the use of worrying? The **only choice is to find out the answers and let us do that**. Let us go through this from the beginning."

"OK. Let me list whatever we need to do now. There are many. To start with, Sevugan, did you upload the logs to Veer's digital container? I need to call Veer again for a quick analysis" Vinitha queried Sevugan.

"What upload madam? I don't recall any instructions" Sevugan gave a puzzled look.

"Yesterday I was busy preparing the report for the health secretary and hence could not focus on sending the logs and exploit codes to Vinod and Veer. It was late when I finished the report and I was tired. Since the log files was too huge in size, I could not send to Veer's email. It had to be uploaded to their digital briefcase. I was too tired to do that. Hence, I wrote instructions to Sevugan and uploaded to his priority task list for the morning" Vinitha wondered if Sevugan was acting smart.

Sevugan learnt to work on Internet and hence Vipul and Vinitha used to assign simple tasks to him and Sevugan liked those tasks. He was happy to do intelligent tasks.

"I have no such instruction for me, madam. Sir, you check my task list. Madam does not believe me."

"Don't act smart Sevugan. I remember very well. I created the task for you and set the target time for completion as 10 AM today and scanned and uploaded it to your Inbox."

"Hold on, Vinu. Sevugan could be correct. How did you upload his task list?"

"In Sevugan's master command console. I am sure I did it. I can show you"

"No need. You are also correct. Sevugan is also correct. You must have created the instruction properly in Sevugan's console, but it will not get updated to Sevugan. The only way now to make Sevugan do any task is to instruct him directly and not through the console."

"How come? We always update tasks in his master console, and he does everything as per the instructions uploaded."

"My dear stupid wife, you put pressure on me to isolate and disable Internet access for Sevugan. How would he synch his instructions and schedules without Internet access?"

"My dear stupid husband, I told you to disable **unwanted Internet access** for Sevugan after selectively whitelisting[1] the required Internet access."

"My dearest stupidest wife, you told me that you cyber security professionals prefer a dumb and stupid robot to a rogue robot."

---

[1] whitelisting – allowing certain access selectively and blocking all others.

"I still say the same. We prefer a dumb robot to a rogue robot. But we don't just like that make everything dumb in the guise of protecting. We are well aware that business has to run, this house has to run efficiently, and I am aware that Sevugan has to get his instructions to run the house efficiently."

"You are giving contradictory instructions. I thought you are upset that I did not block Internet access for Sevugan."

"That is the problem, not just with you, we face with everyone. I am sure I told you clearly, but you listened selectively. We come across this every day in our life. People generally remember only what suits them or what hurts them the most. We are mostly seen as people who hurt their interests." Vinitha gave a long explanation. "You won't believe it; our finance head blocked my salary because I reviewed and removed unwanted and unacceptable privileges enjoyed by him. We are… " Vinitha stopped for a moment midsentence.

Vipul thought Vinitha was going to burst out in fury at Sevugan and himself for this miss but was surprised to see Vinitha bursting out in joy suddenly.

"When did you block his Internet access? Do you remember?"

"Very much. Last Tuesday evening. I remember very well because that is the day your mother tested positive for Covid. I suddenly remembered that I did not do anything about blocking Sevugan's Internet, and you were suspecting that Sevugan could be a reason for spreading the virus to your mother. I was guilty that I did not follow your instruction. I sneaked out from the discussion and immediately blocked his Internet access completely without informing you. Did not get time to go through the instructions for configuring the firewall with so many things happening in the house."

"You see, I am afraid of you, and I obey your instructions to the letter." Vipul added with a smile.

"I remember now. You sneaked out right in the middle of an interesting discussion and you gave the impression that something was 'fishy'"

"That is better. Of course, you could have followed it to the spirit. Father and mother would have escaped Covid if you had obeyed my instruction immediately. Does not matter. But unknowingly you made all my efforts to get conclusive evidence for the past two days futile. Or rather, your action may have the clue to the solution now."

"I agree that I delayed your instruction. But this is quite ridiculous. I get shouted at even if I follow your instructions."

"My dear stupid husband, you could have informed me that you had blocked Internet access for Sevugan. What a stupid person I am! I have been testing Sevugan every hour for the past two days after his Internet access was blocked. How did I miss this important point? Crazy. It is very fair of Vittal to get upset."

"Do you mean to say that he will test positive as soon as he gets back his Internet access?"

"Could be. I would say, a strong possibility."

"You are always diplomatic. You don't need to be diplomatic with me."

"I learnt it the hard way in my profession. It is OK. Let us come to the issue now. I get to understand now that Sevugan is isolated ever since we took the first Covid test report on him."

"One minute. We took the first test report on him the next day after your mother was tested positive. We took his first test on Wednesday but I blocked his Internet access the same day which was Tuesday. Correct?"

"Which means he did not get synch since Tuesday."

"How is he continuing to do his work still?"

"His recurring instructions and downloaded instructions would already be there in his task list. Only new instructions and changes would not come into effect. There is an option to give new instructions without synch. We have to update instructions in his personal console or give voice instructions by prefixing them with the word 'Instruction'."

"I understand but am not interested to give any instruction to Sevugan. Let us piece this together."

"Right. Our intellectual ping-pong."

"First. Why does he require internet access to synch his task list? That happens only from his console software and he can connect to his console system on WiFi" Vinitha started her investigation.

"That is the design of Robogenius NGN. Internet access required to complete the synch. Probably because multiple things happen during the synch cycle apart from synching the instructions. Apparently, synch process does not initiate if internet access is not available to connect to Robogenius' master controller. They have established controllers for redundancy. A log will be sent to the registered phone if the synch process fails and I am receiving logs for the last 4 days" Vipul explained and was afraid that Vinitha would shout at him for not sharing with her the log alert.

"Strange. I must ask Vinod. There must be a purpose to have designed this way. Why do they make it mandatory to connect to their controller for every sych? "

"Even the patch updates happen during the synch."

"But you said you blocked auto-update."

"Yes, I blocked auto-update, so patch updates do not happen during the synch for Sevugan but happens during the synch for many other robots."

"OK. When does the synch take place?"

"We can configure any number of synchs at whatever time. I configured once a day at 8 PM."

"That is even more interesting." Vinitha immediately took her phone and started dialing.

"Whom are you calling? I can explain to you the details. I know everything about synch" Vinitha was not interested in listening to Vipul on what he knew. Not right now. She thought she got the spark and wanted to check on it.

Vinitha called her father and he answered the call on the first ring as if he was waiting for her call. She straightaway came to the question. "When did you and amma take your *panankalkandu* milk?"

"Around 8.30 PM every day. It was not at any fixed time in Madurai. But with Sevugan it was on the dot. He used to come with two cups of *panankalkandu* milk sharp at 8.30 PM every night. He is a good robot, Vinu. Be nice to him."

"I don't need your certificate for Sevugan. I have other important work." Vinitha disconnected the phone.

"You cannot be so business-like, Vinu. They are your parents. Both are in hospital. They are comorbid. You did not even enquire about their health." Vipul complained.

"I know but I badly need the answers now. Never mind. My father will understand. I will explain to him later."

"What next? What are you trying to arrive at?" Vipul was restless.

"What is the time now? *Abra*, tell me the time."

"Time is 10.58 AM Indian time. Do you want me to tell other programmed time zones?"

"No."

"OK. I understand. I can tell you your schedule today. Do you want me to remind you about your schedule today?"

"*Abra*, shut up."

"Hmm. I understand you are upset with me. Don't allow anything to spoil your mood. Be cheerful always." *Abra* advised.

"Vipul, can you activate Sevugan's full Internet access and program the synch for 12 noon today?"

"Do you want to give full Internet access? I have still not gone through the procedure for configuring the firewall. And you said Sevugan is already compromised. Would it create any issue if he is given full Internet access?"

"Does not matter. Give full Internet access."

Vinitha typed Doctor Virus into the phone and the professor's face with the contact details came on the screen. She pressed the Dial button. Vittal Lobo came online.

"Did you get that one positive test on your robot?"

"Not yet, but will get it by 12 noon today."

"Why that specific time?"

"Because it is neither AM nor PM." Vinitha smiled.

"I am just reaching my hotel and am very tired. Got up early in the morning to catch the flight. Can you please update me once you know?"

Vinitha understood his hesitation. She knew that he was still not convinced. She did not want to press further.

"Professor sorry Doctor, can you please arrange a very high-quality Covid2121 home test to be done at my house in another 40 minutes. Please instruct the lab the right procedure to check for virus in robot's skin".

"I can do that. King's Lab in Chennai comes under my portfolio. I would instruct them the right method to run a test on a robot"

"I will arrange that the result will be available in one hour. But ensure that we get a positive test result this time." Dr. Lobo added. He badly wanted this nightmare to come to an end.

"Positive, doctor. I am positive that we will get a positive result this time positively."

Doctor Vittal was totally confused. He disconnected the call.

"I am getting you, you are a genius. No worries. We can configure multiple synchs in a day. We don't need to wait for another 24 hours." Vipul hugged Vinitha and started fiddling with the configuration.

Just then *Abra* started beaming a Red Alert update.

The newsreader started reading the Covid2121 update with a grim face. She announced that the scientists have ruled out the possibility of animal-human or bird-human spread. Covid2121 does not infect any animal or bird. The newsreader also announced that the scientists are working on a new angle if the virus is spread by robots. He added that scientists are working tirelessly and would have an answer soon.

"Not soon, very soon, if they listen to whatever I say." Vinitha beamed.

| SUNDAY, 27ᵀᴴ APRIL 2121

Vinitha suddenly remembered about the *halwa* and *jasmine flowers*. But it was 5.30 AM by then. Dr. Lobo had just left their home beaming and happy. Vinitha forgot her plans for the night in the virus excitement.

"Oh God, I forgot about tonight's fun. Do you remember I said we are starting a new chapter today? I already stopped all birth control measures confident that we would get our license back." Vinitha was full of smiles.

"But we did not take the gene correction treatment. We will be caught in the next test schedule that we have not taken gene correction treatment," said Vipul, the cautious.

"You neither believe in yourself nor your wife. Don't you trust me when I say that I would have taken care of that as well?"

"How?"

"I managed to put-off all the tests for a period of one month."

"How?"

"I disabled the application module which ensures testing the effectiveness of gene correction treatment."

"How can that be possible? That kind of privilege is available only to the Health Secretary. You cannot do that."

"You fool. I ensured that the Health Secretary did that. I don't need to hack for this. He officially disabled." Vinitha laughed.

"How?"

"I was given the right to remove all possible malware codes to cure the problem. I used that opportunity to flag this application as malware and reported that the application had to be disabled until a new application is loaded."

"What will we do when they load the new application?"

"It will take months to do the corrected code and then test it. Remember I must test and clear that before it can be loaded."

"How long will you delay?"

"It is sufficient if I delay for two months. There is no danger if it is activated after two months."

"We will still be caught after two months."

"My stupid husband, gene correction is possible only in the first month. After that no treatment and no testing. We can act as if we are taking the treatment, and no one will test." Vinitha explained.

"Moreover, I have now become a national hero for saving the world from this dreadful Covid2121 and no one will question me until this celebrity status fades away. We will get our job done before that. We should be the first one to get a natural child after this draconian Genetic Correction Act was passed."

Vinitha was very tired but excited and was raring to go. But her newfound superstar status did not give her any time to think about anything other than Covid2121. She continued to get calls and requests for interviews. She had to repeatedly explain whatever she had found out. Her interviews were beamed on the news channels throughout the night. She referred to the Internet and prepared her answers whenever she got some time in between.

The icing on the cake was a phone call received from the Prime Minister's office early in the morning, about 5 AM. Vinitha answered the call with irritation assuming it to be yet another call seeking explanations.

"Call from the Prime Minister's office. The Honourable Prime Minister wants to talk to you, mam. Shall I connect?" The person at the other end asked.

Vinitha was pleasantly surprised to hear the voice of the Prime Minister, that too so early in the morning. She did not know what to say. The Prime Minister's image came on the wall screen.

"Good morning, *beti*. I was briefed about your great service to this nation, rather, the entire world. You yet again proved to the world that India has a solution for every problem of the world. I bow my head in reverence to your contribution. I am very proud of you. Thank you *beti*. You can reach out to me anytime for any support. In recognition of your contribution, I would like to offer you the position of Head of the Cyber Security Cell of the Government of India. Think about it. The Cabinet Secretary will coordinate with you for further details."

Vinitha could not say anything more than, "Thank you, sir. It is my pleasure and my duty."

Vipul asked after the call, "You had lots of apprehensions about the Prime Minister. Has it all changed after this call?"

"I must agree that he has great charisma. We must learn leadership lessons from him. No doubt. But I reserve my comments about my need for 'freedom of expression' and privacy." Vinitha replied.

"I wanted to ask you a lot of questions. Could not get you even for a minute."

"Sorry, Vipul. I am 100% yours now. Shoot."

"I understood that the synch with the home console was the reason for Sevugan to get the virus, but how did he get the virus from the synch application?"

"It is a new cyber-attack. I still don't know the origin of this attack. That is not my job. Cyber investigation agencies are working on the trail. But I found out how the virus came to Sevugan."

"How can a robot get the virus from a cyber attack?" Vipul was curious.

"Do you remember we opted for 'next generation robot' when we purchased Sevugan? These 'next generation robots' are built with human skin-like material to give better sensory perception. This material is known as polyserex. This attack uses the characteristic of this material, remember this is a chemical component, and a particular combination of smell and touch senses to create Covid2121 virus in the skin of 'next generation robots'. The creators of this malware made it to self-replicate through the Internet. The virus would not affect any other component of the robots but they stay in their skin for a period of 30 to 60 minutes and any human coming in contact with the robot within this period gets infected." Vinitha gave the lecture.

"I am still not able to comprehend that virus particles can be created."

"Do you remember the report about Covid19 we heard a couple of days back? There were strong doubts that Covid19 was created in a laboratory in China. If it is possible to create a virus one hundred years back, why not now? Technology has improved over the last 100 years." Vinitha said. The virus has been artificially created and its biochemical characteristics have been programmed into the robot. Just like the aroma, they inject for your *kalpoorarthi* or your *pachakarpooram.*

"I can comprehend that a virus can be created in a laboratory environment but how is it possible for a computer program to create a virus?"

"That is the ingenuity of the creators of this program. They manipulated a particular combination of smell and touch components in polyserex chemical to create the virus. Cyber researchers are still identifying the details. I keep getting updates. My job got over after handing over the necessary evidence to prove that the virus is being created by this program. This malware pattern defied the conventional pattern of all anti-malware programs. Anti-malware vendors have now fixed their code to identify and prevent this malware. We had to stop 'robot synch' by a government decree until the updated anti-malware code was released."

"I understand that NGN robots are vulnerable because of this stupid chemical polyserex. But why did this happen to Robogenius robots only?"

"Because an ethical hacker identified a 'remote code execution' vulnerability in 7.4.0 version of Robogenius and published it. The attacker used this vulnerability to inject the code into the robot."

"We should have upgraded to the new patch. But I remember you said the malware would have come even before Robogenius upgraded the version for the first time."

"Yes. Unfortunately, hackers are faster and many a times they manage to finish their task before a patch cures the problem. But it is still important to upgrade to the new patch quickly."

"I understand and I will never forget, my cyber professor! But why nobody, even the Robogenius team could not find out that their robots were hacked?"

"Because the creators of this malware were very smart, like me. They made sure to delete all traces of the malware and all the indicators of compromise."

"Amazing. I am happy that my wife is a global hero now and the Head of the Cyber Security Cell for the Government of India."

"I have still not decided if I should accept the offer."

"Why not?"

"Leave it now. Enough of virus talk, human as well as computer. Let us focus on our task. Let us create our child quickly before a new generation of virus hits. It is possible that WAVE 2 of Covid2121 could come in a different format." Vinitha hugged Vipul.

"I decided to seduce you. I purchased *halwa* and *flowers*. But they are lying untouched in the refrigerator." Vinitha smiled.

"I don't need *halwa* or *flowers* to seduce you. Your intelligence is more than enough of an aphrodisiac."

"It is only 6:00 AM. The night is still young." Vipul kissed her and it was a passionate kiss.

EPILOGUE

Vinitha took up the offer and became Head of Cyber Security Cell to the Government of India. She worked very closely with the Government of India and was instrumental in drafting a progressive Cyber Security Policy for the Government of India. The family relocated to Delhi.

Air Wall was built successfully across the entire border of India in two years. Vipul was named the best Project Manager of Air Wall project. Many in the company mumbled that he got the recognition due to his wife's proximity to the government. Vipul's company received more orders from the Government of India. Nobody could guess the rationale behind the sudden rise of that company.

Sevugan was very happy that he also became famous overnight and started respecting rather revering Vinitha. Vinitha and Sevugan became terrible duo. Sevugan learnt cyber security analytical skills from Sunitha and helped her in her work. Sevugan learnt cyber security on his spare time instead of Bhagavad Gita and Tamil.

Varad and Vijaya managed to go to moon and return safely.

Vipul and Vinitha got their son early 2122. Routine tests indicated that the child's match with the approved 'Gene Pattern' was only 42%, well below the average value. Controllers questioned them about the variation but the case was dropped courtesy Vinitha's access to corridors of power.

Government of India further tightened birth control measures and 'Gene correction' regulations. There were murmurs of protest but everyone got used to the new restrictions within 3 months.

Government of India passed a regulation making it mandatory for all the robots including house robots to be shipped with an approved anti malware software and made it mandatory for all owners to mandatorily assess the security of all robots minimum once a year. It was rumoured that Vinitha played a major rule in drafting this regulation.

Robogenius continued to be the market leader of robots despite bad publicity from Covid2121 fiasco.

T Jaganathan
Author
COVID 2121
T JAGANATHAN
BUY NOW
CONTACT US